FRAGILE NIGHT

Stella Pope Duarte

Bilingual Press/Editorial Bilingüe
TEMPE, ARIZONA

ISBN 0-927534-71-1

Library of Congress Cataloging-in-Publication Data

Duarte, Stella Pope.
    Fragile night / Stella Pope Duarte.
      p.   cm.
    ISBN 0-927534-71-1 (alk. paper)
      1. United States—Social life and customs—20th century—Fiction.
    2. Hispanic Americans—Social life and customs—Fiction.
    3. Hispanic American families—Fiction.   4. Family—United States—
    Fiction.   I. Title
    PS3554.U236F7   1997
    813'.54—dc21   97-23080
                                        CIP

Cover design by John Wincek, Aerocraft Charter Art Service
Back cover photo by Carl Hayden High School photography students, 1997

Acknowledgments

Partial funding provided by the Arizona Commission on the Arts through appropriations from the Arizona State Legislature and grants from the National Endowment for the Arts.

FRAGILE NIGHT

Bilingual Press/Editorial Bilingüe

General Editor
    Gary D. Keller

Managing Editor
    Karen S. Van Hooft

Associate Editors
    Karen M. Akins
    Barbara H. Firooyze

Assistant Editor
    Linda St. George Thurston

Editorial Board
    Juan Goytisolo
    Francisco Jiménez
    Eduardo Rivera
    Mario Vargas Llosa

Address:
Bilingual Press
Hispanic Research Center
Arizona State University
P.O. Box 872702
Tempe, Arizona 85287-2702
(602) 965-3867

CONTENTS

For my children,
Vince, Monica, Deborah, and John Mark,
my four miracles

*Patience, weary traveler, darkness in
the end will reveal the light.*

WHAT LA LLORONA KNEW

"Where are you going now?" Luis's voice pierced the room's dark silence.

"I'm checking up on Mama," Elena whispered. She felt an apology rising in her throat but managed to swallow it down before it got to her lips. She moved quickly to the side of the bed, letting her feet find her thongs in the dark. With one hand she smoothed down the wrinkles of her white cotton nightgown, catching a patch of dry skin on a down stroke. With the other hand she patted her husband's bare shoulder.

"I'll be right back. Just go back to sleep."

"Yeah, right. La Llorona never rests."

Elena ignored the remark and walked out of the room, shutting the door behind her. She paused outside the door, a wooden barricade that separated two parts of herself, the dutiful wife from the loyal daughter. She strained, listening for Luis's voice, but heard only the door's thud as she shut it.

He had to make a comment. Always. As if the whole thing was her fault. As if she staged her mother's problems on purpose to make one more job for herself. One more task, after cleaning cracks and crevices in split linoleum floors and faded formica counter tops that, in spite of all her efforts, regained their forlorn look seconds after they dried. The task was endless, much like the task of wiping her kids' runny noses, except they hardly ever dried. Life was the same song played over and over again with the volume out of control. There were sounds Elena pretended not to hear, memories she tried to forget, then forgetting tried to remember again. Still, she heard herself singing the same song all over again. She wanted to change places with Luis, wander into the house after work and demand a meal. Slump down on the couch and watch TV, snoring loud enough to start the neighborhood dogs howling.

Elena walked down the narrow hallway past the kids' bedroom, listening for the crowded, soft breathing of three children piled onto one bed. At the end of the hall she saw the thin line of light under her mother's bedroom door. Her mother's lamp was on. It was one of those nights. Nightmares were arrows pinning her mother's thoughts like darts on a target, sure of their mark, knowing that no matter how many times they struck they would find their way to her heart. Elena remembered the nightmares, pesadillas, that dissolved an ordinary woman's dreams into insanity. Why her mother? Her skinny, hunchbacked mother who never even watched horror movies.

She remembered herself as a child watching her mother drink manzanilla at the kitchen table at odd hours of the night, holding onto her Bible, reading, skipping pages. At other times her mother wandered the house, pacing, pacing, sometimes walking out into the dark night as Elena stood helplessly at the door.

"Mama? Where are you going?" Elena rubbed her eyes, pressing out the tired feeling with her fingers as she would watch her mother walk out the door. She explained it all to her teacher the next day as a headache, a stomachache, an itchy back.

"Go back to sleep. Don't follow me." Her mother's voice was final, thrust at her like a hand-me-down dress.

"Stop crying!" Elena had yelled back. "Stop making me think you're crazy!"

"Go back inside. Your father will get mad." Her mother's voice had no ups and downs, no signs of life. The nightmares had taken over again.

There was no one to help. Elena's father, after many fights over his wife's nocturnal trips, gave up on trying to stop her and learned to sleep and snore whether she was in bed or not. After his death his wife continued her nightly walks and forgot she had ever had a husband waiting for her to get back to bed.

"I guess she wants to run around like La Llorona," Elena's father said in mockery. "Who am I to stop her? Nobody ever stopped the real Llorona."

The infamous tale of the real Llorona was ingrained in the hearts of all the kids in the family by the telling and retelling of the notorious crime she had committed against her own children. Yes, she had actually thrown her two small children into a raging river—drowned them—and all because of a man.

Stories of this grisly murder retained the same theme, with changes in details to better fit the local village or storyteller. The plot was always the same: a beautiful, haughty woman fell deeply in love with a handsome, dashing no-gooder and suffered his unfaithfulness. He had set out to marry the proud, vain girl just to show that he could win her, to prove his machismo—for he was a ladies' man and was faithful to no woman. After finding out about his affairs with other women, the young wife went mad with jealousy because her unfaithful husband loved only other women—and his two children. Well, she would show him. She would hurt him by taking away his children forever!

So intense was the pain of her husband's betrayal that La Llorona turned against her own children, not realizing that in killing them, she herself would die. Her death was sudden and came immediately after the unspeakable act, probably as she ran up and down the river bank trying to retrieve her children from the turbulent water. She fell into the river gorge and broke her neck on a huge rock.

Her name and shame grew with each retelling, until no one knew what her real name had been. She was destined to bear the name "La Llorona" until the end of time, for she weeps every night for the loss of her children.

"So, you see," Tío Pepe would say to Elena and all the children who gathered around him to hear the tale, "See what happens to girls who think too much of themselves? They get the worst in life. And I have to warn you that La Llorona is so crazy—entirely loca—because of what she did, that she goes out every night to look for her children."

Then his voice would drop to a whisper, causing the terrified children to move in even closer. "You might see her some night, crying for her children, flying in the air, wearing a long, white shroud. And if I were you, I would run, oh so fast, as fast as I could all the way home, because La Llorona doesn't even remember what her children look like." He would end in a loud voice: "And she might think YOU'RE one of them!" His finger pointed in a menacing way at each one of them, and all the children jumped together and held on to each other for dear life, pledging to protect one another from La Llorona for the rest of their lives.

"My mother, the twentieth-century Llorona," said Elena out loud as she opened the door to her mother's room.

Her mother was already up and ready to begin her nocturnal walk. Her thin bathrobe hung closely around her frail body, making the jagged bones of her shoulders and back stick up under the faded material. She was tying up her silvery hair in a bun, one bobby pin here, one bobby pin there, preparing for a long night of walking.

"Going somewhere, Mama?" Elena asked impatiently. She thought of Luis alone in the dark bedroom.

"No, mi hija, I just can't sleep tonight and thought I'd go check to see if there's a moon out. Go back to bed; Luis will get mad." Elena heard a hint of emotion in her mother's voice. Maybe the nightmares weren't as bad now. There could be no more excuses. Enough was enough. The disobedient parent had to be stopped, put back to bed, her eyelids forced shut, the light turned off. La Llorona would not be allowed to walk tonight.

Elena opened her mouth to say, "Mama, I've told you how dangerous it is for you to walk around, even in the backyard. Violence, Mama, don't you understand violence? Anything can happen to you."

Instead, she was disarmed by her mother's hands. White knuckles stuck up in rigid formation as she clutched her pink handkerchief. There was something about the helpless way her mother's eyes dropped to look at her hands that made Elena change her mind.

"I'll walk with you, Mama," she said, surprising herself.

"What about Luis? I don't want any trouble."

"Mama, that man *is* trouble all by himself. It won't matter. He's mad all the time anyway."

"Just like your father."

Elena, two heads taller than her mother, linked arms with her and the two walked out through the back door and into the yard. Outside there was a moon—a big, silver moon—full and high in the sky. A few sparkling stars peeked out from behind thin, white clouds. Elena's dark hair trailed behind her, catching the gleam of moonlight, and her mother's hair shone ghostly white in the eerie light. Night smells of grass and the penetrating perfume of orange blossoms greeted them.

Crickets were chirping everywhere, rubbing their skeleton legs together, searching for mates. Nighttime shadows hovered over the yard and patio, making even the children's worn-out toys beautiful in the half-light. The huge mulberry tree, with branches that grew over the rooftop, stood stately and silent in the center of the yard, its branches moving gracefully in the night breeze.

The first time around the yard, the women said nothing. Elena felt the light warmth of her mother's arm encircling her own. Was her mother really La Llorona? If that was true, that made her La Llorona's daughter. Elena's mother answered her daughter's thoughts. "I walk because it brings me peace. If I didn't, I would have gone crazy years ago."

"You, Mama? Crazy over what?"

Her mother sighed. "Ay, mi hija, we all have a story to tell, and since you've decided to join me tonight, I'll tell you mine."

Her mother started the story as they began a new circle around the yard.

"It all happened during the Mexican Revolution, when there was so much fighting all over Mexico that it was hard to tell who were your friends and who were your enemies. My father often brought revolutionary generals, captains, and common soldiers to our house for rest and food. Of course, in payment they would give our family protection. I was only about fifteen years old at the time.

Among these visitors was a captain, and I will use his name for the first time in over sixty years. His name was Lorenzo de Tapia Murillo! He was a tall, muscular man with light skin, a marvelous smile, completely straight teeth, and a perfect profile. And such a sweet manner!

One night, as Captain Lorenzo and others joined us in our evening meal, I was sent to help serve with the other women but was told not to talk to any of the men. I was young, and according to everyone I was the most beautiful of my father's five daughters. This Captain Lorenzo kept watching me all night, but never once did he approach me or try to touch me.

As the night wore on, the men drank more and more tequila. In fear of the men's lust, my older sisters began hiding themselves wherever they could find a secret place. I also hid. I climbed one of the giant trees on my father's ranch, and very quietly I settled down, prepared to stay there all night.

I guess this Captain Lorenzo was spying on me, for before very long there he was under the tree calling up to me. I could see that he was quite drunk, and I was afraid. I must stay up here, I said to him. Those are my father's orders. But I am the captain, he called back to me, and I order you to come down at once!

Unsure what to do, I obeyed him, as any child would obey someone in authority. As soon as my feet hit the ground, he grabbed me roughly and spun me around, holding me in his arms and kissing me hard. I fought him off, but the more I tried to get away, the harder he held me.

It was quite dark out where we were, and I screamed several times to try to alert someone to help me. But what with the music and singing still going on, no one heard me. He tore at my clothing, threw me down on the grass, and raped me."

Elena stopped, her legs suddenly paralyzed under her. She saw before her the images of the rape. Tears gathered in her eyes as she faced her mother in the dim light. She was ready to speak, to give voice to her pain, when her mother's voice rang out sternly.

"Keep walking!" She gripped her daughter's arm. "Keep walking; the story's not over!" Elena struggled to keep pace with her mother, feeling like a small child who must match her steps to her mother's or be lost forever. There was no time for tears.

"That's better," said her mother. "Now you're ready to hear the rest." She took a deep breath, letting it out quickly in a puff of air that opened the path before them.

"I didn't even know what to expect when the captain threw himself on me. I thought he just wanted to see my body. That's how innocent I was. So violent was his attack on me that it seemed as if he had torn my body in two. Finally, he put his arms over my body and fell asleep on me in a drunken stupor. I remember trying to push his body off of mine, but I was too weak and eventually passed out.

When I woke up, I found that it was daybreak, and the captain was still asleep in his drunken stupor, half-hanging over my body. I used my remaining strength to push him off and sat up to put on what was left of my dress. Then I stumbled over rocks and splintered tree limbs until I reached the house.

My father, also coming out of his drunkenness, was first to greet me. He immediately began calling me names. Lifting me up by the hair, he called me a whore and told me that I had shamelessly given myself to a man.

I cried out to him to look at my bruises and blood, but he shoved me into the house, slapping me and shaking me hard. My mother sat at the kitchen table, preparing mole for the day's meal, and when she saw what was happening, she became a helpless child herself. She never could stand up to my father's violence. She began rocking back and forth, looking straight ahead and humming a little tune. She never once looked at me, as my father forbade her to comfort us in any way when he disciplined us. I remember that when it was over, I looked at my mother and saw tears streaming down her face. My poor Mama—may she rest in peace! My father just looked at her rocking back and forth and said that she was in her own world again, a lunatic for sure.

There was no way for me to tell my father who had done this horrible thing to me, for he himself would have been shot for accusing one of the revolutionary heroes of such a deed. A woman simply did not stand a chance. By the next day the revolutionaries were gone, including Captain Lorenzo, who didn't bother to look at me again. Indeed, he stayed away from me the rest of the day.

Within a month's time I found out I was pregnant. My father was enraged. Now he had to contend with the evidence that proved his own inability to protect me from such violence. How his conscience must have stung him! Yet he showed me no mercy. He decided to send me away, to put my shame far from him."

The pieces of the story Elena's mother was telling fit perfectly into the night, into the dark cradle that swayed under the burden of pain. Her voice now became urgent.

"When I was near the end of my pregnancy, my father told me that he was going to send me to a certain captain and his wife who had befriended him and who knew of my situation. How glad he was, he said, that this good man and his wife would give me a place where I could have my baby in secret. Yes, mi hija, the captain turned out to be Lorenzo de Tapia Murillo!

I was packed off and sent with one of my brothers to the captain's house and told that I was to serve them as a maid. I remember that the captain's wife had a daughter about a year old. When I realized where I was going, I cried and cried, saying that I would go anywhere else, even to the moon if necessary, but not there. My cries fell on deaf ears, and I ended up going there anyway."

Elena's mother stopped the story. The abrupt silence between the two women resounded like a drumbeat. She began again slowly in a voice she used when she told a deep, dark secret to the priest.

"In spite of all I suffered at the hands of the captain, I found, to my complete surprise, that I was in love with the man! Don't misunderstand me, mi hija. I beat myself up inside over this and tried to convince myself this wasn't true. But when I saw the captain kiss and hug his wife, I died a thousand times in agony, thinking that if he hadn't been drunk and reckless or I so young, perhaps it might be me he was kissing and hugging. Can you imagine such a thought? The captain, for his part, didn't treat me cruelly. In fact, he hardly spoke to me at all, and at times I caught him staring at me, for he knew just as well as I did whose child I was carrying.

Finally, the day came when I delivered my baby. And what a beautiful baby boy he was! The captain's wife and another woman helped me. I was so young, innocent of childbearing and the ways of women, yet I fell in love with that baby boy as I held him briefly in my arms. He looked so like his father—the straight profile, the light skin and hair. I say that I held him briefly, for before the hour was up, the baby was taken from me and sent to another house where he would be cared for until his return to the captain's home. He was to be raised as the captain's son and not mine!

Within two days I was returned to my father's house, where my mother received me with weeping. To this day, I believe my mother knew the whole story. I can only tell you that I was filled with grief, and it became so great that I decided to take my own life. One night I ran out to the river at a time when it was running wild and full. I didn't know how to swim, as my father never permitted the girls to learn. I jumped in, not knowing that two lovers were hiding in the bushes behind me. When they saw me jump in, the woman screamed, and the man jumped in after me and dragged me back to shore.

They knew who I was because our town was small and we all knew each other, so they took me to my father's house. I remember waking up to my father slapping me and calling me a whore, which was his favorite name for me.

After this suicide attempt my father had everybody in the house watch me. He didn't want my death to dishonor him further in the eyes of others. It wasn't until months later that he finally allowed me some freedom.

It was at this time in my life that I learned to walk at night to relieve my grief. The night understood what I had been through. I walked around the house in the dark, gazing at the moon and stars as I am doing now, and just as I am doing now I traced a cross in the air, blessing my son wherever he was and sending him my love. And I sent my love to his father, forgiving him though my heart ached with pain. The pain of what he did to me and the pain of loving him still.

One morning my father caught me walking and said I was crazy like my mother, like La Llorona. He was scared of ghosts and thought maybe La Llorona had taken up residence in my body. Can you imagine? After that he left me alone. It took three years for him to come up with somebody who would marry me, for everyone knew I wasn't a virgin. He finally found someone who said he would take me off his hands and make me a respectable woman. That man was your father, a fat drunk that not even the girls from the bar wanted. My father was grateful for anything I could get. The only good thing your father ever did for me was to bring me here to Los Estados Unidos, where all of you were born."

Elena's tears fell down her face and onto her nightgown, blurring the full moon and the stars that had traveled across the sky.

"Did the walking help you, mi hija?" asked her mother, poking Elena playfully in the ribs.

"Yes," said Elena, "I guess it did."

"See, we have something to learn from La Llorona. She knew that only the night could endure her pain. Now we know." Then they both giggled in spite of their tears.

"Let's go back inside, mi hija," said Elena's mother. "It's dangerous out here."

LOS GEMELOS

Jorge knows there's trouble in José's life. Big trouble. Trouble enough to sound a wail in his identical twin brother over two thousand miles away. This isn't really mental telepathy, Jorge considers. It's more like when he and José were kids swimming in the pool at the local park. They popped out of the water together, gulped air into their lungs, then raced for the bottom of the pool. Last one back up had to take out the garbage for a week. It was nearly always a tie.

This time it feels different. The race is urgent. Already Jorge's left arm feels numb. His heart is telling him it must pump for two instead of one.

The call comes on Wednesday.

"Jorge, it's Claudia. When can you come?" There's a muffled sob.

"I already booked a flight. I'll be there tomorrow night. Where is he now?"

"Intensive care. The doctor says maybe two months, if we're lucky . . ." More sobs, blowing into a Kleenex.

"It's OK, Claudia. I'll be there." They hang up with no goodbyes. Jorge sighs, keeps his hand on the receiver. His left arm sends a warm sensation through his body. He pulls out his wallet and looks at the plane ticket. It tells him he was right, there's no turning back. An open space in the clouds yawns at him. He's already traveling in time, lost in a sea of white clouds. It's the Atlantic reaching for the Pacific. Windblown, tempest-tossed, he's disappearing, heading west, a tiny speck going back to the beginning. It has to happen. He reaches for the receiver and dials Karen's number.

"What's wrong with your arm?" asks Karen, meeting Jorge at the door of her condo. She circles his neck with her arms. Her forehead comes up to his collar bone. Jorge bends down to hold her briefly, stroking her silky, blond hair. She smells of the lavender soap he gave her for Christmas.

"My arm?"

"Yeah, you're dangling it."

"It feels a little numb." He sits down on the couch after removing Stanley, the Siamese. He smells stir-fry.

"Want something to eat?" Karen sits next to him, stroking his leg with her hand. "What's wrong?"

"I'm going to San Diego tomorrow. José's sick. I mean bad. Terminal. Claudia called me tonight." He glances at Karen, sees her look away, watches her put her hand back on her lap.

"How long will you be gone?"

"I'm not sure." He avoids her eyes and stares intently at the tapestry hanging on the wall.

"Is it over between the two of you?"

"It's been over for years. What are you talking about?"

"Oh please, don't even start, Jorge." Karen stands up and cradles his chin in her hands. She gently rubs the back of her hand against his face.

"This is a real test. You won't fight over Claudia any-more, will you? I don't want to lose you." He sees flecks of light in her eyes, radar signals, warning. Your gringa with the eyes of a cat, his mother always said.

"I'll talk to you when I get back," he says. Karen looks stunned.

"Aren't you going to stay tonight? Jorge, please stay." He feels lousy, swallows hard, wants to say yes but says no.

"I've got some thinking to do." He knows Karen understands space, individualism, not being co-dependent. He doesn't want to admit it to himself, but Claudia's voice got stuck in his ear and now Karen's sounds Chinese. Her hair is the wrong color. Her eyes are intrusive. Yesterday they were only small lanterns watching him, loving him. Now he's not so sure.

Jorge thinks of Karen as he boards the plane. He searches for a seat—by a window or near the aisle, it doesn't matter as long as he's not by a talker. He slumps into a seat in the back next to a man with a hearing aid. He tries to camouflage himself by assuming the shape of the seat.

Karen wanted to come with him, had already called the airlines and put herself on a waiting list for a flight three hours after his. He had had to convince her, talk to her for over half an hour. It would be too much for his mother at a time like this. The image of his mother's face enters Jorge's mind. Juana's worried brows, the corners of her eyes crinkled, scrunched up to study him, to try to understand why he isn't married. "You and that gringa living in sin." With that attitude there was no possibility of doing a sleep-over at Mom's. "The saints would fall headfirst to the floor," Juana told Jorge after meeting Karen for the first time. "Esa gringa, she doesn't even know how to make the sign of the cross!"

Jorge tries without luck to get some sleep on the plane. He wants the metal ship to lull his senses, to make his disappearance less obvious. He's following this time. Before, it was always José following him. Right out of Juana's warm gunnysack, the little sucker, trying to be first even then. But Jorge made it by two minutes at least. Regrets came later. The feeling of being followed stayed with Jorge. He couldn't shake it off, couldn't make José stop following him around until they met Claudia.

Jorge looks out the window, remembering the identical Christmas gifts and look-alike Easter baskets they received each year. "So they won't be mad at each other," Juana said. Jorge was mad anyway. He wanted his gift to be different, to be the best.

He would have changed the holy medals once and for all if he had known Claudia would fall in love with José. Another one of his mother's ideas. When the twins started school, Juana had pinned a medal of the Sacred Heart on Jorge and a medal of the Blessed Mother on José so she could tell them apart.

"I should have kept the Blessed Mother on," mumbles Jorge.

"The what?" asks the man next to him.

"The medal."

"Did you win a medal?" asks the man, cocking his head to the right.

"Yes, a Silver Star," says Jorge. He feels bad lying to him. The man reaches over quickly and shakes his hand.

"Congratulations, son. Welcome home."

"Thank you."

Jorge smiles, closing his eyes because now he's a war hero. Before he was only somebody's twin brother. The one with short sideburns. José had the long sideburns, Elvis style. His father's idea. Noé was clever, a great barber, but he failed his boys. The sideburns idea didn't work for long. He forgot who had long sideburns and who had short ones, and sometimes the twins had jagged sideburns because Noé stopped in midair trying to figure out who was who.

"I should have kept my sideburns long," Jorge says.

"You suffered burns?" asks the man.

"Yeah, over sixty percent of my body," Jorge says in a loud voice. The people across the aisle turn to look at him to see if they can see any scars.

"God bless you, son," says the man, reaching over again and shaking Jorge's hand. Jorge feels he's playing games, except José's missing. The crazy games they played. He almost laughs but stops himself. Wouldn't be appropriate for somebody as severely burned as he was.

The games, the games, the stupid games of childhood. Innocent enough. Not many could play them, not as effectively anyway. Jorge remembers running in one door and José running out the other. "You already finished cutting the grass?" his father asked in surprise. "Yep, all done." And his father paid him two dollars while José was still outside sweating over the lawn mower.

It got to be too much for Jorge. He wanted out of his skin. "Leave me alone, you brat," he shouted at José. "Get your own friends. Stop following me around." It got so bad for Jorge that he almost had a fight with his eighth-grade teacher because he kept confusing him with José. "I'm not him. Get it through your big fat head!"

"I'm not him" was Jorge's battle cry, but later he wished he was. Wished it most when he met Claudia in the school cafeteria. She was sitting next to his brother, casually eating french fries, when Jorge edged his tray in next to José's. Claudia's tiny, translucent face was as delicate as the face of a porcelain doll. She was thin, too thin for her height, yet her huge, dark eyes lit up her face, making her body appear full and sensuous. Jorge sat unblinking. He glanced around the cafeteria, wondering if anyone else had noticed the heavenly vision before him. Sunlight streamed in through the windows, catching the light in her dark, glossy hair. All he could think about were knights in shining armor and damsels in distress. He had the urge to fall on his knees at her feet. This was his princess. He looked over at José and saw a moonstruck expression he had never seen before on his brother's face.

By this time Jorge had made it, had changed himself to look more like somebody else. He was no longer the tall, slender artist, the daydreamer who doodled squiggly lines on page after page of Big Chief notebook paper. Portraits had been José's favorites back then, and desert landscapes were Jorge's. He was now a thick-framed football player, shoving extra calories down his throat every chance he got. Claudia had no problem telling them apart. "José's brother? Yes, I see it now." And she studied the same face, the perfectly pressed ears, the hazel eyes, the nondescript bump on the nose, the dimple on the left cheek. "So, you are twins!"

Jorge couldn't wait to get to the gym that day to tell José about his crush on Claudia. José was cool, practicing basketball.

"I want that girl," Jorge said as they both jumped together. "I want her bad."

"Want her? The question is, does she want you?" asked José.

"Then she wants you? Is that what you're saying?"

"Let her decide," answered José with a smooth smile.

Without warning Jorge jumped on José and beat him down to the hard wooden floor of the gym.

"Don't mess with me, pendejo!" he growled, pinning his brother between blows. "I told you, she's mine!"

Who knew how it would have ended had not the coach run out to stop the twins, grabbing Jorge and holding him until he calmed down. And he had to calm down again when he found out that Claudia had chosen José, the artist like herself, his gentleness matching her own, his creative ability equal to hers. Jorge was now on the sidelines watching his brother run ahead of him with his princess.

"I should have beat him up when I had the chance," Jorge says out loud.

"They beat you up?" asks the man.

"No, I beat him up,"

"Who?"

"The man who torched me," says Jorge, looking serious.

"Good," says the man. "He deserved it."

Arriving at the San Diego airport the man shakes Jorge's hand again and claps him on the back.

"An honor, son, to sit next to a war hero."

"My pleasure," says Jorge.

"I'm at the airport. I'll get to the hospital by taxi."

"I'll wait in the lobby," says Claudia. "Is Karen with you?"

"Who?"

"Karen."

"No, I don't want Mom to have a heart attack."

"I didn't tell José you were coming. I didn't want him to get his hopes up too high."

"He knows I'm here," says Jorge. "Believe me, he knows." He shakes out his left arm, feeling it go numb again. There's a rush of movement in his head, a space Jorge knows is José's. He hangs up, forgetting again to say goodbye. He wipes his mouth with his hand after putting the receiver down, trying to get rid of the energy Claudia sent him over the phone, impulses electrified by her voice.

Walking into the lobby Jorge spots Claudia sitting in an armchair. She is wearing a soft pink outfit that clings to her curving outline like suede. She's gained weight over the years, adding fullness to her sensuous body. There is the old urge in Jorge to fall on his knees at her feet. Instead he strides confidently towards her, his hand stuck out in front of him. She bypasses his outstretched hand and hugs him, crying softly. Jorge catches the smell of her, the musk mixed with clean skin that is Claudia. Tears gather in his eyes.

"Thank you for coming," she breathes in his ear. "José will be so happy."

Jorge breaks the hug and puts both hands on Claudia's shoulders, standing her at arm's length.

"Are *you* happy?" he asks.

"Me?"

"You don't have to answer that. I'm sorry."

"I'll answer it," she says. "Yes, I am. What is José without you? Think about it. Do you know what it's done to him, living apart from you all these years?"

Jorge's arms drop to his side. He looks past Claudia.

"Jorge, look at me," she insists.

"What for? I'm not here for that. I'm here for my brother."

"Stop running, will you?"

"Claudia, this is a hell of a time to talk about all this."

She puts her hand on his arm. "Jorge, don't pull away. There's so much you don't understand. So much you don't want to know." He meets her eyes, obsidian infused with light. He shudders, his knees weakening.

"Are you OK?" she asks.

"Sure," he says in a loud voice. "I'm fine. Nothing to it. Seeing you again and visiting my dying brother all at the same time are the easiest things I've ever done."

"Now you're talking crazy."

Claudia buries her face in her Kleenex.

"Look, let's forget about all this, OK? I'm sorry. When will I say it enough?" He puts his arm around her shoulder. "What floor is he on?"

"The fifth," she sobs.

Jorge's skin feels alive under his clothes. He fingers the edge of his turtleneck nervously as they walk to the elevator. He watches people get on, and a faint hope comes over him. The elevator will be filled to capacity, and he will have to let Claudia go up by herself. As they board Jorge notices a "1000 pound capacity" sign posted. No chance.

Claudia continues to cry softly.

"Claudia, stop. You're making me feel worse."

"I'm not trying to. I've never tried to do anything or be anything I'm not supposed to be. Not like some people I know."

"I quit trying to be a jock years ago. You know that. As a matter of fact, I'm now a member of the New Jersey Fine Arts Commission."

"You are?" Claudia wipes the last of her tears away.

"I've even gone back to painting. I'll bring some of my work next time."

"Desert landscapes?"

Jorge laughs. "I've advanced to forests and oceans by now."

Claudia smiles.

Jorge battles an urge to grab her and pin her in his arms. Instead he concentrates on following the elevator light as it blinks its way up to the fifth floor.

He walks with Claudia to José's room. They stop at the door and Jorge runs his hand through his hair, then over the new stubble of beard on his face. This is worse than seeing Claudia again.

Walking into José's room, Jorge gets a whiff of an unmistakable odor, not a stench but more a vapor over everything. Life clinging by its fingernails. Jorge is shocked by his brother's appearance. José's thin, bony body is gray and lifeless. Jorge tiptoes in, watching his own face on the pillow. Please, God, give me strength, he whispers. He bends down and kisses José's forehead, watching his eyelids flutter and open, first in confusion, then in recognition and joy.

"Knew you'd make it, bro," José says. His voice sounds hoarse, trembly. "I knew you wouldn't let me down."

"I booked the flight two days ago," says Jorge, making himself laugh. He bends down and cradles his brother in a gentle hug. "That's one good thing about us. We always know when something's up."

"Is your left arm numb?" asks José.

"Yep. How 'bout yours?" They laugh together.

"What time is it?" José asks as he motions Jorge to help him sit up. "It looks dark outside."

Jorge looks out the vertical strip of window onto the city below. Building lights twinkle in the dark. He catches a glimpse of his brother's deathly reflection in the glass and Claudia at his side, holding his hand. Quickly he blinks back his tears.

"Took me a while to get here from Jersey," he explains.

"And whose fault is that?"

"What? Another guilt trip? And I just got here." Jorge draws a chair up to the bed.

"Mom's never been able to get over it, your moving so far away."

"Damn, I should have stayed in Jersey." Both twins are silent.

"Tell him, Jorge," says Claudia.

"Tell him what?"

"That you're a member of the New Jersey Fine Arts Commission."

"¡Órale! My own brother rubbing elbows with the yuppies!" The twins clasp hands. Flat palms, thumbs up, curled fingers, tap on the knuckles—the homeboy handshake.

"Couldn't fight you forever," says Jorge. "Didn't want to, anyway." He puts one hand over his brother's.

"Why don't you go get Mom and the kids," José says to Claudia. "She'll be in heaven to know that Jorge's here. And the boys, you haven't seen them in two years. They're already big. Steven's nine and Nick's twelve. Wait 'til you see them, Jorge."

Jorge looks out the window again, remembering the births of his nephews, the excitement mixed with bitterness. "Yes, bring them. I want to see them," he says. "And tell Mom not to wear black."

Watching Claudia walk out, Jorge feels the knot in his throat loosen and the coil of energy in his stomach unravel.

"You should've seen the guy on the plane," he says. "I had him going, thinking I was a war hero."

"No shit. He believed you?"

"All the way to San Diego."

"Were you cara palo, to the very end?"

"To the very end."

"Wish I had been there; I would've loved it. Our games were better when we played them together, que no?"

"Yeah, we had some good old times."

"And now?" asks Jorge.

"Can't play hardball anymore," says José. "But I got a little something going."

"You got me out here."

"How'd you know?"

"Did you make yourself sick to bring me home? Is that it? I've heard of crazy things like that. People twisting their minds to do all kinds of things."

"I got creative in my old age."

"Is this a game?" asks Jorge indignantly.

"It's the only way I can still play," says José. "And there's more. You gotta do something for me."

"Oh, no," says Jorge, looking into his brother's sunken eyes. "I love you bro, but don't ask me for that."

"You know what I want, don't you?"

"Yes, and the answer is no."

"Gotcha bro. You can't deny a dying man's request."

Jorge stands up. "I've got a life. I've got Karen."

"That's easy. You don't love her. We both know who you love. Well, now you can have her."

"Just like that? Because you say so?" There's anger in Jorge's voice.

"Cut the dramatics," says José impatiently. He strains from his position on the bed, edging closer to his brother.

"Jorge, you've got to help me," he says urgently. "I can't stand to think of some stranger trampling over Claudia and trying to father my kids. You don't know how much this is making me crazy!"

"You must really be crazy! Are you telling me to take over Claudia like she's some kind of possession that I can now claim? You're wrong, bro. I know you're sick, but you don't have to be psycho too."

"I'm no psycho! You would do the same thing I'm doing right now. Think about it. Claudia fell in love with the kind of man I am, and who else is more like me than you? There were even times after you changed back to yourself that I didn't know if Claudia was in love with me or with you, and it didn't matter anymore."

"It matters to me!"

"That's why you're gonna do what I say. For once." Tears start a trail down José's face. His head sinks back into the pillow. Jorge reaches for a Kleenex to wipe his brother's tears, then dries his own. The words have cost José his strength, leaving him shaking, his teeth chattering. Beads of sweat form on his forehead. He locks eyes with Jorge, and the answer is caught in the air between them, invisible hands sealing the bond, making them more identical in death that they have ever been in life.

"I always wanted to marry a princess," says Jorge after a pause.

"I've missed you so much," whispers José. "God, I've missed you."

FRAGILE NIGHT

It's usually a good idea when you wake up in the middle of the night to have some warm milk sprinkled on top with a little cinnamon to help you get back to sleep. That is, unless you have other reasons for staying awake, in which case the cup of milk will not help you, not one little bit.

"Never a good idea to hold bitterness in at night," Abuelita Minerva told Alma. "No, not at all. Because bitterness will compound anything you have suffered during the day, and make things unbearable for you at night."

Alma often wondered how Abuelita got her odd name. The name Minerva always made her think of a Greek goddess. It didn't sound Spanish to her.

Everybody said Abuelita was a sprig off the old tree, one in a long line of wiser-than-thou women who inhabited her side of the family. Alma was her favorite, the one she taught to crochet, play solitaire, and spit tobacco. (The last only until her mother found out!) Uncanny how Abuelita read Alma's thoughts from across the room. Alma figured she got messages from her rosary beads. Abuelita was in the habit of spying on her large family from her high-backed chair in the corner of the living room while she prayed her rosary. At odd intervals she came out with the most absurd statements. She tested her children like she tested a hot iron with a wet finger to see if it was ready.

Sometimes they were ready and sometimes they weren't. Usually Alma wasn't ready; not then, anyway.

Alma got a little closer to the truth about herself one day, although at the time she was drowsy and complacent, letting her breasts fill up with milk for Alfredo Jr.

It happened on Christmas Day. The scene lived on in Alma's mind for the rest of her life, one of many scenes that played themselves in her head over and over again, each time seeming more real than the time before until they towered over her, commanding her to look at them when she didn't want to. Alma was used to running. Even in her dreams she ran. From phantoms, from knife-wielding butchers who pursued her relentlessly. In real life it was the opposite, she wore lead shoes.

Everyone had just finished eating Christmas dinner when Abuelita asked, "You don't love Alfredo, do you, Alma?"

Alma peered into the corner of the living room where Abuelita sat, surprised at how clear her voice sounded. "What?" she asked. Abuelita's head barely came up to the purple doily on the chair's headrest, and she didn't miss a beat on her rosary beads. Alma shifted the baby in her arms, readjusting her nipple in his mouth.

"You heard me, mi hija. You don't love Alfredo."

Alma looked through the sliding glass door leading out to the backyard where all the men were drinking. Just at the moment Abuelita said, "You don't love Alfredo," he glanced up at Alma and saluted her with a tip of his beer can and a smile.

"I have his baby, Abuelita. What are you talking about?"

"That doesn't matter," Abuelita said. "That has nothing to do with love."

At that moment, Alma's mother, Gloria, walked into the

room and heard the last of Abuelita's words. "What's all this about love?" she asked.

"Nothing you would understand," answered Abuelita, looking past her.

"Oh, and I suppose you would?" said Alma's mother with her hands at her hips. "Who died and made you the world's expert in love? I suppose," she went on indignantly, "that my staying with Efraín for the last thirty years doesn't prove love?"

"Son de la misma pluma," responded Abuelita.

Gloria's face contorted in anger. "And who do you think puts a roof over your head if it isn't Efrain?"

"And who put a roof over his head when you first married him and he gambled all his money away for ten years?. Shall we go on?"

Alma put one finger over Alfredo Jr.'s ear, the one not squished into her breast, so he wouldn't wake up with all the shouting. Tía Blanca sided with Gloria and Tía Lola took a solid position with Abuelita against the cunning Efraín. It was good that dinner had already been served or somebody would have probably rammed a hot tamale down somebody else's throat. As it happened, Tía Lola decided to leave first, rounding up her five kids and piling their assortment of cheap Christmas toys into her car. "Some women are beyond help," she muttered.

"No respect for el día del Santo Niño!" cried Gloria.

Everyone forgot about Alma, and Abuelita went on praying her rosary. Alma wanted to put the baby down and run to Abuelita, sit at her feet, and ask her to explain love. Before she married Alfredo, she had never asked Abuelita a thing. She thought she knew it all. She thought she had love curled up in the palm of her hand. Every now and then love's volcano threatened to erupt from between her fingers. Alma clenched her fist tighter and laughed.

Alfredo was under her spell. Even Cecilia couldn't attract his attention. Her spiked heels clicking and sexy legs swaying Marilyn Monroe style didn't catch Alfredo's attention, or so it seemed to Alma. She should have learned how to pray the rosary, then maybe she would have gotten to the truth!

Three times Cecilia had passed between Alma and Alfredo, on purpose, that night at Sal's house when they first met. Alfredo had looked through Cecilia like she was a ghost and looked at Alma like she was the only woman in the whole wide world. A heady trip for Alma, so heady it got heavy. That's when Alma started wearing lead shoes. She was satisfied with the attention Alfredo gave her, happy with what it meant to belong to him. The clink of a metal yoke linking her fortunes with those of Alfredo's seemed perfectly normal to her. There was power in being possessed.

"The perfect couple," said Sal. "You two were made for each other." He said this with a sneer that wasn't obvious to Alma. If anyone knew Alfredo, it was Sal. He knew Alma posed no threat; una vieja Alfredo could wrap around his finger. There might even be some left over for him.

A beautiful couple, everyone had said. Never mind that Alfredo was a womanizer. He was ready to change. Ready to call it a draw, to end the card game, hands down.

Alma accepted Alfredo's proposal of marriage less than a year after they met.

"He reminds me of your abuelito. Muy macho," said Abuelita as she and Alma prepared dinner one evening.

"Alfredo's not like that, Abuelita!"

"I said the same thing about your abuelito when I got married. See this bald spot?" She pointed to a small circle of clear scalp at the top of her head. "Your Abuelito dragged me by the hair when we were first married."

Alma looked down at the tomatoes she was chopping. "That was in the old days, Abuelita. It's different now."

Abuelita carefully spooned boiled beans into a frying pan of hot grease. "Men and women are still the same, mi hija," she said. "Only true love makes any difference."

In spite of Abuelita's disapproval of Alfredo, Alma married him on a cold, windy day in November. The wind blew so fiercely that Abuelita had trouble keeping her lace veil on her head.

As the young couple walked out of the church after the ceremony, the mariachi started to play. The sky opened up like a giant waterfall and rain fell in torrents. The bridal party was drenched. Alma's bouquet blew down the street and got caught on a chain-link fence.

"Que mala suerte," said Abuelita, running for cover under a tree. "All this bad luck. If the marriage starts this way, imagine how it will end!" She took off her veil and used it as a handkerchief to wipe her tears away. The last thing Alma saw as the car whisked her away to the reception hall was Abuelita crying into her veil.

Two years after Alma was married, Abuelita died. By then Abuelita's eyes were two sunken circles set into the bony ridges of her face. She lay neatly tucked in bed, unable to move even a fingertip, but her eyes followed Alma around the room. Her rosary was twisted through her fingers, but she didn't talk to the beads anymore, unless she was doing it in her head.

Alfredo was unconcerned, because he knew Abuelita gave him dirty looks every chance she got. There was nothing Alma could do about that outside of covering Abuelita's face. Alma's mother went into a fit. "She's doing it on purpose because she knows I like him." Alma felt uneasy because she wanted Abuelita to give her a blessing before she died, if only with her eyes. She wanted Abuelita to look softly at Alfredo, like she did at her.

"I love you, Abuelita," Alma whispered. Tears started in Abuelita's eyes at the same time they started in Alma's. Alma bent down to Abuelita's ear and asked for her blessing. Abuelita moved her lips and managed to say, "May God have mercy." Alma tightened her grip on Abuelita's hand, reeling from the words.

Alfredo was standing next to Alma, but he didn't hear what Abuelita said. It wouldn't have mattered anyway. He only believed in himself and in the things he told himself were true. If he hadn't thought about it, it wasn't true, even if it was staring him in the face. For instance, when Alma had seen him kissing Cecilia on New Year's Eve and complained that it didn't look like a Happy New Year's kiss to her.

"You're imagining things," he said. "How could I love anyone else? You're having my baby."

"You had your hands all over her."

"She's just a friend."

"Friends don't kiss friends on the mouth!" Alma shouted. It was the first time Alfredo slapped her. It took Alma by surprise, not like later when she learned to move faster. Alfredo Jr. sat straight up in Alma's womb.

Alma raised her hand to hit him, but he caught it in midair.

"Don't you even try it, you little bitch," he said.

"So now I'm a bitch! Before I was your pregnant wife." He looked like he was going to hit her again but clenched his fists instead. He went easy on Alma that time because they hadn't been married long enough. It wasn't the pregnancy that yanked his hand back from further violence; he proved that later when Alma got pregnant with Andrea. That time he kicked Alma so hard, Andrea almost came seven months early. What saved her were Doña Carolina's hands. She was the curandera who lived in the projects. She knew how to stroke Alma's stomach so the baby would want to hold on. Then she gave Alma a drink of water from Lourdes to help the baby get over her fear.

"Es un perro," Doña Carolina said flatly about Alfredo. "You should leave him for good, mi hija. I remember your Abuelita couldn't stand him."

After a while, her mother couldn't stand Alfredo either, but she told Alma he'd get better.

"Be patient, mi hija. Look at your father. He beat me for the first fifteen years of our marriage, and now he's as meek as a lamb."

"Yeah, after Mario broke his jaw," Alma said. Mario had turned fifteen just in time to catch hold of his father's shirt as he ran for cover after knocking Gloria to the ground. Mario ripped all the buttons off his father's shirt, and there was Efraín with his ribcage showing. Mario didn't hesitate. He swung his pitching arm full-force straight into his father's jaw. It was the first and last time Mario had to prove his point.

Blundering her way through years of marriage, Alma learned to make darkness her companion. She took to sitting in a dark corner of the living room when Alfredo was out drinking. Even before Sergio was born, she was already in the habit of making herself as still as the night. Invisible forces surrounded her. Shadows swayed before her eyes, converging, dissolving, weaving a snake charmer's spell over her. Night's fragile weave lay a welcome mat at her feet that suspended her, levitating her like a saint. Alma broke all the rules. Old rules that held her fast, that grounded her when she should have been borne up by love's wings.

Alma learned to speak in gibberish. Disjointed sentences

came from a voice she didn't know in the light. The honest voice. The one that told her the truth, that invited her to sit in a corner of the room with a rosary tangled in her fingers. Alma spoke often with the beads, and they talked more to her than she did to them. Abuelita was there. Alma sensed her near. She saw her eyes; not the sunken ones, but new ones glittering in the dark.

Confessions ran long. Alma talked to God. She wanted Him to look at her, to make her understand love. Her head was so full of Alfredo, God had to reach Alma by dreams, where Alfredo couldn't catch up to her. Alma found out what she was looking for—by fighting a whore who pranced boldly into her dreams claiming Alfredo as her own. For years the woman bore Cecilia's face, until the day Alma challenged the real Cecilia at Sergio's baptism.

It all happened so quickly Alma didn't have a chance to think about it until later. It was really quite simple. Cecilia walked slowly by in stretch pants and a blouse that plunged down to her navel. Alma couldn't resist the temptation to put out one foot and trip her. Cecilia landed with her face in her plate of barbacoa and beans.

"I'll get you for this!" she yelled at Alma.

"Get me now, you little whore!" shouted Alma. She put down one-month-old Sergio and stood ready for action. Her blood was still pumping hormones left over from childbirth in crazy, uneven spurts. Alma felt strong, a cross between Lois Lane and Superman.

Alfredo pushed Alma aside and helped Cecilia to her feet. He brushed the barbacoa and beans off Cecilia's clothes and apologized to her.

"Alma's a little psycho," he said. "She needs a good beating."

Alfredo tried a good beating when they got home.

He pushed Alma up against the wall, slapping her hard.

She fought with all her might while eight-year-old Alfredo Jr. ran to the neighbors for help. By the time the cops got there, Alma had managed to get away from Alfredo and was headed out the door.

The whore in Alma's dreams disappeared when she admitted the truth to herself, loosened the laces on her lead shoes, and got closer to the spirit of Abuelita Minerva. Alma ran her fingers over the rosary beads and knew the woman in her dreams was herself. Worse still, she didn't even collect money. A whore at least demanded payment, but what had been her excuse for staying with Alfredo?

These nights Alma sits alone with her daughter asleep in her arms. Darkness hides them like two babies wrapped in towels, newly bathed. The pores of Alma's skin open. She blooms in secret. So many nights of tears and gibberish to come back to Abuelita's words, "You don't love Alfredo, mi hija." Alma nods in the dark, listens to the phone ringing. Picks it up. Alfredo.

"Hope you're happy." she says.

"I'm not."

"Cecilia isn't enough?"

"Not like you. She's fat and ugly."

"You waited too long."

"Listen to me, will you?"

"I never loved you," she says.

"I can't believe that."

"Believe it."

She puts the phone down, winks at Abuelita Minerva in the dark, and prays her daughter learns to know her heart.

THE REMEDY

Probably if Panchita hadn't gotten hurt that Saturday, none of this would have happened, and this story might never have been told. But the truth is, Panchita did get hurt that Saturday afternoon by a rock that hit her right on the side of the head. The rock grazed the tiny temple area where her hair was smoothed down without a wrinkle to form one of the two braids that hung down her back. According to her father, one inch further and it would have hit her right on the temple, and who knows if Panchita would have ever risen from the ground again. A horrible thought—to lose a young child all because her older sisters fought like animals day and night.

"¡Como animales!" cried their mother when describing the viciousness of her two daughters' quarrels and fights. "If they had claws, they'd have no eyes at this very moment!" she would add in dismay, dabbing away at the tears that glistened in her eyes when she thought of the problems brought on by Nene and Amada.

Nene was one year older than her look-alike sibling, having reached the ripe old age of ten. She was also the first-born of the Contreras family and Señor and Señora Contreras were still kids themselves, new to the task of raising children. The young couple had tried separating the girls by sending them to different corners of the same room. They had tried taking their dolls away from them and making them apologize to one another with a kiss. They had even tried giving them extra chores so they had to work together to get everything done. Nothing changed the girls' behavior in the least, and indeed their quarrels with one another seemed to increase. Also at the mercy of the girls' quarrels were six-year-old Tito and four-year-old Panchita, the youngest members of the Contreras family.

No one had a clear idea as to when Nene and Amada had started quarreling. It was even said that one year old Nene, upon seeing her newborn sister in the cradle, had let out such a furious whine that the neighbors next door had come over to see if their dog, Lumbre, had bitten anyone else that day. They saw Señora Contreras holding the enraged Nene in her arms to stop her from reaching into the cradle and making a short end of her sister's entrance into the household. And so it began. As Amada grew older, she was able to return Nene's attacks by hitting her sister on the head with a rattle, and as she grew still older, by spitting food at her or breaking things and letting Nene take the blame.

From the moment the girls opened their eyes to the moment they closed them to sleep for the night, there was trouble between them. To make matters worse, they slept in the same bed, because the family could not afford another bed, and even if they could, there was nowhere to put it in the small house they lived in, the fifth one in a row of houses with tangled yards that comprised their vecindad.

Typically, the girls began quarreling even before they rose from bed, arguing over who woke up first and who had dreamed more dreams. They debated over who had kicked who during the night and compared bruises, for they slept opposite each other, one pillow on each end of the small bed. This gave them an excellent opportunity to shove their feet into one another's faces or slam their heels expertly into thighs, legs, stomachs, or chests.

The question they contended with each morning was who would get up first.

"I'll get up first," said Nene, who slept curled up at the edge of the bed.

"Oh, no you won't!" cried Amada. "I've been pushed up against the wall all night."

The girls never settled this argument, and they eventually rose together in a twisting of blankets, legs, arms, and feet.

The day Panchita was hit by the rock had been a typical one for the Contreras family, except for one added dilemma. All the quarreling and fighting by Nene and Amada had reached a fever pitch at school and the director of the school, Señor Justino de la Torre, had sent the following letter to the girls' parents:

Estimados Sres. Contreras:

I am sorry to report that your daughters, Nene and Amada, have continued with their quarrels here at school in spite of all we have done to try to stop them. Señorita Pacheco has taken a paddle to them on many occasions and has done the best she can to try to beat some sense into them, but they remain as hardheaded as ever.

Today, they fought in the cafeteria at lunch and caused one of the children to slip on spilt milk and land on his back. It is a wonder he is not crippled due to the fall.

I will no longer tolerate your daughters' quarrels at my school, for they are a danger wherever they go. I would like to see you both in my office at 8:00 A.M. sharp on Monday morning to discuss this very serious matter.

With all due respect, may I suggest that a visit to a priest may be in order.

I remain at your service (possibly),

Sr. Justino de la Torre, Director

"What have I done to deserve this?" wailed Señora Contreras after reading the letter. "Imagine what people will say! And to think that I was an honor student at the same school!" In her mind's eye, she already saw mud splattered all over her good name.

"I've worked so hard to send these girls to school!" bellowed Señor Contreras. "And for what? So they can make a fool out of me!" He imagined everyone laughing behind his back, wagging their fingers, accusing him of not being man enough to take care of his own children.

The reason Señor and Señora Contreras received the letter at all was because Panchita had whispered in her mother's ear that Nene had something in her pocket from school that she was hiding. Señora Contreras looked up and saw Amada peeking around the corner of the kitchen door.

"Who told you?" she asked Panchita, and the child pointed to the disappearing Amada.

"Amada, come here!" her mother ordered. Amada slinked back into the kitchen and stood with her head bowed before her mother. "Haven't I told you not to get your little sister in trouble? Do you suppose she can defend herself against Nene?" Then angrily she thrust a big wooden spoon into Amada's hand. "Stir the chili while I go and find out what this is all about!"

Señora Contreras didn't have far to go. She quickly spotted six-year old Tito making a dive for the oleander bushes and suspected that Nene would be close by. She knew Nene and Amada used the younger children as pawns to add strength to their quarrels. They would send the younger children out as spies, Tito siding with Nene and Panchita siding with Amada.

Señora Contreras couldn't find Nene no matter how loudly she called for her. In the kitchen, Amada let the chili burn because she kept running to the kitchen door to see what was happening.

Later that afternoon, full-fledged war broke out in the backyard. Rocks flew everywhere over hastily made shields of cardboard boxes, until in one deluge of stones, Panchita lay wounded on the ground, moaning and holding the side of her head. Señor and Señora Contreras ran out, frightened at the sight of their youngest child lying on the ground, bleeding. And they both knew who was to blame.

"That's it!" roared their father, "I'm taking these girls to Doña Cuca today. She'll know what to do."

"No, Papito, no!" yelled Nene and Amada in unison. "We'll be good."

They knew that to go see Doña Cuca was to undergo whatever treatment she thought best for the illness or condition at hand. Doña Cuca was the neighborhood curandera, and she knew everything there was to know about illnesses, herbs, ointments, mysterious powders, and concoctions. She knew how to massage a person's body to bring health back to anyone except those who were already dead. She also knew at least one hundred prayers by heart that she recited as she massaged the body or administered medicines. Her treatments were never questioned, nor were there ever any unsatisfied customers.

Señor Contreras picked up both girls, one under each of his lanky arms, which, incidently, were also a cause of argument, for the girls quarelled over whether his arms were the same length or not. Nene said they were, and Amada said that his right arm was longer than his left one. Ignoring their cries, Señor Contreras put them both in the back of his old Ford jalopy, and away they went to Doña Cuca's adobe house at the end of the winding alley.

Upon arriving, Nene and Amada followed their father past Doña Cuca's chicken wire fence, which was overhung by vines that produced a delicate, pink bloom. Then they marched straight through Doña Cuca's rickety gate that was crisscrossed by two pieces of wood held together by an old, splintered latch.

Once inside the yard, the three stood on the hard-packed ground under more vines that extended from one wooden trellis to another, creating a patio for Doña Cuca's tiny house. And under the patio, with a gray cat curled at her feet, sat Doña Cuca on an old, flowered arm chair. Her white hair was smoothed back from her face, forming a bun at the back of her head, and she was dressed all in black in honor of her husband, who had died over twenty years ago. In her hands was a Bible, also black, that she held up as she read, her light brown eyes scanning the pages carefully as she read out loud:

"Unless you become like little children, you shall not enter the Kingdom of God." As she uttered the words, she saw Señor Contreras standing in front of her with his two girls.

"Ah, the innocence of children, Señor Contreras. If we adults could have hearts as pure as theirs, we would all go straight to heaven!"

"Forgive my interrupting your reading, Doña Cuca," said Señor Contreras apologetically. "But these two young girls you see before you have hearts that are far from pure. And to tell you the truth, because of all the quarreling and fighting they do, who knows but they may be headed straight for hell!"

"¡Dios mío!" cried Doña Cuca, making the sign of the cross over herself. "May God in His great goodness forbid such a thing!"

Señor Contreras explained to Doña Cuca why he had come. He stood between the two girls, one hand placed firmly on each shoulder. Nene and Amada stood silent, looking down at their shoes while their father told her about the quarreling and fighting, about Panchita's wound, about his wife's distress, and most of all about Señor Justino de la Torre's letter.

So great was Señor Contreras's anxiety as he stood in the presence of Doña Cuca that he was tempted to throw himself at her feet, pleading like a beggar with tears in his eyes for a remedy for his daughters' quarrels, but he contained himself, for he was a man after all, and what would Doña Cuca think if he acted that way?

"And they look so like angels!" mused Doña Cuca, looking at the girls closely. "Do please come in, Señor Contreras. I think I have the perfect remedy for them."

With that she led them slowly into her house, which consisted of only one room with a hard-packed dirt floor, an ancient bed against one wall, three old, tattered chairs, a small stove with cooking utensils, and two cupboards filled with row upon row of bottles, each containing an unnamed liquid. An imposing antique bureau topped with holy pictures, statues of saints, and burning veladoras completed the room's furnishings. Over the bureau hung an enormous ceramic cross entwined with a blue, glass-beaded rosary that sparkled in the glow of the candlelight. The aromatic fragrance of peppermint, spearmint, garlic, and olive oil permeated the room's atmosphere.

"Siéntense," said Doña Cuca, pointing to the three tattered chairs. She began rummaging through one of her cupboards, looking for the liquid she needed for quarrels. She finally brought out a tall bottle filled with a whitish-yellowish liquid with a bay leaf floating in it. Then she approached both girls with the bottle and a large spoon.

"It is unfortunate that you girls with the faces of angels have chosen to act more like devils, making everyone suffer around you," said Doña Cuca. "But there is an easy remedy for you, and it will begin here and now. Which one of you starts these quarrels?" she asked.

"She does!" said both girls, pointing each to the other.

"Just as I thought, neither one wants to be the first to stop. And it is so important to want to stop quarreling for the cure to begin. Perhaps one dose of this medicine will help you to at least want to stop."

Nene and Amada each had one hand over her mouth, aghast at the thought of having to take such a large spoonful of a liquid that might taste like poison. The spoon resembled the large one their mother used to stir the chili for tamales at Christmas. But there was no getting away, and their father was present to force the medicine down their throats if need be.

"Nene should be first because she is the oldest," said Doña Cuca. She poured the medicine carefully into the spoon, then sprinkled white powder over the mixture and said, "In the name of the Father and of the Son and of the Holy Spirit," and forced the spoon into Nene's mouth.

For a second Nene looked as if nothing had happened. Her eyes were fixed steadily on Amada as she gulped down the liquid. Then a look of sheer agony came over her face. Her lips turned every which way, worse than when you eat lemon with chile and salt. She coughed and gagged and held on to her throat while she spun around, landing on Doña Cuca's bed headfirst.

Without even pausing to see the outcome of her first patient, Doña Cuca was ready with the next spoonful for Amada, who ran to hide behind her father. Her father danced around a bit trying to catch hold of his daughter and finally secured her for Doña Cuca. With her father holding her and Doña Cuca half choking her with the spoon, Amada, screeching and screaming, had the dose of medicine forced down her throat. Her reaction was a duplicate of her sister's, except that Amada went one step further and bolted out the door, treading on the gray cat's tail on her way out and making it rear up and scratch her on the leg.

Doña Cuca ignored this behavior also and gave instructions to Señor Contreras on how the medicine should be taken.

"Make them responsible," said Doña Cuca in warning. "Let them give the medicine to each other just before bedtime, Señor Contreras. Then bring them to me next Saturday, and if they are still quarreling and fighting, I will have another bottle of medicine ready for them."

The first thing that happened after climbing into their father's old Ford was that both girls agreed that the medicine had tasted like fly's legs mixed with lizard's juice and the tongue of a horned toad. This was the first time they had agreed on anything at all! Tears of relief appeared in their father's eyes, and he patted the bottle of medicine that lay beside him on the front seat.

Señora Contreras was sitting on the front porch with the wounded Panchita on her lap and Tito at her side when her husband and daughters returned home. She watched in silence as they walked towards her. She held Panchita closer with one arm and encircled Tito with the other.

"We have it!" said her husband happily. "The remedy for

quarrels!" And he lifted up the tall bottle, which gleamed like a jewel in the setting sun.

Señora Contreras looked in disbelief at the three of them, expecting Nene and Amada to tackle one another to the ground any moment.

Instead Nene said, "Mama, we'd like to help you make supper."

Señora Contreras looked as if she would collapse when she heard Nene's voice sound so calm and reasonable.

"Of course," she said, smiling hesitantly. The younger children stood back clinging to each other, unsure what to do next since their leaders were acting so strangely.

That evening was the most blessed the Contreras family had yet experienced. Señor Contreras even pulled out his old guitar and strummed away, playing a few chords to accompany himself in song. Tito and Panchita played together like an ordinary brother and sister, with no one to egg them on to trouble.

At bedtime, after receiving their nightly blessing, the bottle of medicine was placed in Nene's hand and the large spoon in Amada's hand. Alone in their room, the two girls, in identical striped nightgowns, looked suspiciously at each other.

"You're the oldest. You go first," said Amada.

"Oh, no I won't! I was first at Doña Cuca's," said Nene.

"Well, I suppose one of us will have to report that we are quarreling again," answered Amada, a wave of fear already sweeping over her.

"You wouldn't dare!" said Nene in great alarm. "Please, Amada, you wouldn't, would you?"

"I suppose you think I like this poison myself, do you? Of course I wouldn't tell," said Amada.

"Then who will be first?" asked Nene.

"Not me," said Amada.

They both eyed each other darkly. Then Nene held up the medicine bottle, and Amada held up the spoon, and each girl's face turned pale with the memory of the taste they had suffered earlier in the day.

So they decided that night that neither should take the spoonful of medicine. They agreed instead to keep a secret between themselves and the rose bush growing outside their window, for it was the rose bush that received both spoonfuls of medicine! In fact that night was the most peaceful the girls had ever shared.

In the morning the girls said not a word to anyone about their secret and continued to agree on everything, constantly remembering that Doña Cuca had many medicine bottles available if trouble continued.

On Monday morning Señor and Señora Contreras met with Señor Justino de la Torre to discuss their daughters' behavior at school. They related that the girls were under the care of Doña Cuca and that she guaranteed relief from quarreling. They reminded him that she had never had an unsatisfied customer. He agreed, remembering his trips to Doña Cuca and his own screeching and screaming and dancing.

The girls were thus allowed to remain in school. And throughout the day, if one felt like quarreling, the other had only to point to her mouth in a gesture of what would happen if trouble started all over again, and the quarreling would stop before it began. The rose bush outside the girls' bedroom window, to everyone's surprise, began growing at a phenomenal rate and soon covered the entire window and half the outside walls with gigantic red roses.

And in his pocket so he wouldn't forget, Señor Contreras carried the remedy for quarreling as written for him by Doña Cuca: *In secret suffering is found peace.*

THE MANGO

A half-eaten mango lying on the kitchen table attracted Carmelita's attention as she turned on the kitchen light. She reached absently across the counter for a glass to get a drink of water.

Just like me. That's me if I ever saw me. Cut open, half used, and ready to be thrown out. At thirty-five years old and still living alone, the matronly Carmelita felt like the mango almost every night. Every now and then she suspected there was sweetness somewhere inside her, but on this night, like all others, there was no one to convince her there was.

I must be going crazy thinking of myself like this, she thought, gazing momentarily at her reflection in the small kitchen window above the sink. She looked at her plain, brown face, small mouth, and eyebrows too thick for the rest of her face. Her hair hung to her shoulders in straight, dark strands that opposed Carmelita's attempts at curling and waving. The only thing she liked was her nose, which curved in a smooth slope, separating her hazel-brown eyes. Otherwise, as everyone said, Carmelita was feíta and gordita, yet wonderfully kind, yes, with a charming smile and hands always ready to help those in need.

In fact, helping those in need was why Carmelita was living alone in a small frame house behind the big house of the Andrés family. She was employed as a teacher for the only first grade at la Escuela Primaria de General Zapata. Carmelita considered this charity work, for the wages she made in the small country school couldn't keep a flea in clothes and shoes. That's why the community employed the unmarried and loners, especially those considered feí-tas, who had no hope of ever getting married and would devote themselves to the tasks at hand.

And tasks at hand were never wanting for Carmelita. If it wasn't her work at school and helping set up for every extracurricular activity that the school sponsored, it was helping church groups make menudo, tamales, pan dulce, and whatever else they needed for get-togethers after Sunday masses.

Besides that, there were the endless favors asked of her by the huge Andrés family that consisted of eight children. Carmelita could barely keep track of all the children's com-ings and goings to her house and their constant playing, fighting, and running back and forth through the yard.

She thought of them as "the brood," yet she still couldn't bring herself to refuse Señora Andrés when she came over with a child, straddled over one ample hip, for her to watch.

"Carmelita, will you take care of Manuelito for me?" Eufemia Andrés asked every other day. "I'll only be a minute at the market."

The minute extended to hours, sometimes even past din-ner. Then two or three of the other Andrés children came over to keep nine-month-old Manuelito company and to see what Carmelita had in her refrigerator. Carmelita couldn't bring herself to ask them to leave. After all, their parents were letting her live cheaply in the crumbling old shack. Although, to tell the truth, the rent payments Carmelita made from funds left by her mother after her death were still far more than the shack was worth.

Carmelita cradled Manuelito's chubby body in her arms because he refused to be put down. Aching from the burden she carried, her arms eventually became numb and felt like two dead weights connected to her shoulders.

"Even *you* tell me what to do," murmured Carmelita to the baby. And she smiled because it wasn't his fault, either.

On top of all this, Carmelita had to suffer the complaints of Eufemia Andrés, who fought constantly with her short, wiry husband because he left most of his wages at the local bar in payment for drinks and gambling debts. Carmelita witnessed their arguments from her small kitchen window, for their fights often advanced out into the large backyard with its haphazard assortment of old cars, tattered furniture, unused tools, and broken-down bicycles.

As Carmelita sat quietly at the kitchen table holding the half-eaten mango in her hand, she thought of what her life had become one year after her mother's death. Before this time, at least, her purpose for living had been secured by caring for her mother. After her mother's death, with no husband or living brothers and sisters, she remained alone and marked out as one who needed to be looked after. It was difficult at times for others to remember she was present at family and community gatherings. She seemed to blend in with whomever happened to be near her, a disposable item, wanted for her skills as a teacher yet misplaced in her life as a woman. She was to be pitied, una mujer dejada, a spinster, a reminder of the worst that could happen to a woman.

Carmelita remembered two Sundays ago when she had sat with other women at a party for yet another baptism, and the wife of the local storeowner, Señora Yáñez, had said to her, "Well, Carmelita, when do you think you'll be getting married? By now your Prince Charming should be in need of having his clothes washed!"

Everyone laughed, and Carmelita, with Manuelito on her lap, good-naturedly replied, "Oh, I'm perfectly happy the way I am. I'm so busy I don't even have time to look for a man."

"The clock is ticking away, and you know that men don't grow better as they get older, if you get what I mean," said Señora Yáñez with a wink.

Everyone laughed again, and the women began making suggestions to Carmelita, naming divorced men they knew, or others whom they humorously described as womanizers or drunks or men with such bizarre behavior that no woman would seriously look at them. And they giggled and clapped as they considered each man and the possibilities for wedded bliss, making up stories of what it would be like to be married to this one or that one.

"Marry Anastacio," suggested her cousin Bernice.

"You mean Frijoles, don't you?" said Bernice's sister. "That's what he's full of, and that's what he smells like too!" She laughed holding on to her sides as she thought of Frijoles and Carmelita as husband and wife.

"Seriously, now, don't you ever want to have children?" asked Señora Yáñez, lifting a small glass of tequila to her lips. "Oh, I know they have caused me these white hairs, but really I wouldn't have wanted it any other way."

"She has to hook Frijoles first!" said Bernice, and everyone roared with laughter. Carmelita laughed too, burying her face in Manuelito's soft, milk-scented neck to avoid seeing the faces that only reminded her that life had passed her by.

When Carmelita considered the dead-end scenario of the single woman, she felt like throwing up. As a child she had heard everyone say, "Es feíta. You're lucky Señora López. She'll stay by your side and be a faithful daughter."

Everyone said the same thing, not minding that

Carmelita was standing in the room listening. And her mother counted her blessings for having such a caring daughter, one who had gotten her education and now would be able to support herself. Her mother closed her eyes in peace for the last time knowing that her feíta would do well on her own, for her chances of finding a husband had long been exhausted.

Carmelita felt tears starting at the corners of her eyes as she remembered her mother, her last link to a real family. She had never felt more alone, more misplaced than she did tonight. She shook her head vigorously from side to side, trying to shake off syllables that wanted to form a shout in her mind. Without thinking, she took a kitchen knife in her hand and sank its sharp edge into the mango. She sliced off a piece and raised it to her lips.

Her eyes blurred with tears as she accepted the sweet juice of the mango into her mouth. Eating around the soft, green rind, she felt comforted by its familiar flavor, and her need to cry was held back by the mango's distinct taste in her mouth. When she swallowed the mango, Carmelita's strength was renewed and her senses were aroused in a way unknown to her before.

"Dear God, strengthen me," she prayed. Then, as if in one mighty movement, caught between her prayer and the mango's sweet taste, Carmelita made a vow to herself. "I'm leaving this place if it's the last thing I do!" she shouted.

Anger moved in Carmelita like an electric shock that nearly knocked her off the chair. Anger at all the humiliations she had endured for so long. Anger for all the times she played the role of servant for family and friends. Anger that not even her esteem as a teacher seemed to make up for the vicious way people looked at her as a non-person, a woman who belonged to any household because she had none of her own. A woman to be pitied, pobrecita, who had never made love, never borne children. Worst of all was the anger she felt at herself for never speaking up, for allowing others to run her life.

Behind the first wave of anger came another and another that collided inside Carmelita's body, rushing straight for her mind to become thoughts she never dreamed existed within her. And the furious pace of anger was so unlike Carmelita that her hands began to tremble and she put the knife down, afraid for the first time of what her own actions might lead her to do.

First of all, she wanted to run out into the night, bang on the door of the big house, and give the Andrés family a piece of her mind and tell them what they could do with their poverty-stricken old house and their endless brood of children. Then she would take off running, her figure ghostly in the night, to el director's house and tell him what she thought of his mismanaged school and his ignorant decisions that never seemed to be what she hoped for. She would shout at him for all the times he failed to listen to her and for all the times he treated her as just one more woman who had to do as he said. Then, out of respect for her mother, she would run to the cemetery and tell her that her feíta was leaving forever. Then she'd return to the crumbling old house at once to pack her clothes and leave—for who-knows-where, but she would go—tonight!

As the energy of anger continued its collision course in Carmelita, she heard a knock at her door.

"Who is it?" she shouted. Her voice filled with rage as she thought of having to deal with one more Andrés family member.

"It's me, Enrique," answered a man's voice.

"I don't know an Enrique!" she yelled back. "Go away!"

"I know you don't know me, but if you open the door I'll introduce myself," said the man's voice.

Before this night Carmelita would not have dared speak to anyone in such a tone, much less to an unknown man at her door. No, she would have brought her voice under control and swallowed her rage, although it would have tasted bitter indeed and not like the taste of the mango at all. She would never have allowed the passionate display of anger that had just exploded inside her like fireworks on Independence Day.

Carmelita stood up in a frenzy, wanting to get to the door to tell the intruder to leave at once. As she opened the door she didn't even bother to smooth her hair or look to her bare feet under her blue cotton robe. Nothing mattered but this one vow she had just made and the victory of escape that she sensed close at hand.

"Forgive my bothering you," said the tall, robust man that she faced. "I'm a cousin of the Andrés family and have been knocking at their door with no answer. Would you be able to tell me where they are tonight?"

"I don't know," said Carmelita carelessly. "To tell you the truth, I don't care."

"Again, let me apologize for this interruption," the man said. "My name is Enrique Salazar, and I've come from El Paso to leave some clothes and things for my cousins. Is there any way I might be able to wait for them either at their house or perhaps here? I wonder if you aren't the señorita that teaches at the school. They said, well they . . ."

"I can imagine what they said," said Carmelita with a smirk. "They never have anything good to say about anyone."

Enrique hastily surveyed Carmelita from her round face to her bare feet, and he thought her charming and a bit comical in her anger. "May I come in, please, señorita, maybe have a drink of water?" he asked.

"Call me Carmelita," she said, moving from the entrance to allow him to come in.

Carmelita filled a glass of water for Enrique as he sat at the kitchen table. Still feeling the energy of anger inside her, she didn't allow herself to form an apology for her unjust treatment of the man who now sat at her table. In one instant, she noticed his slightly balding forehead, the brown moustache and sideburns slightly graying at the ends, and the dark brown eyes that now looked into hers. He wore a plaid shirt neatly tucked into his Levis, which were held at his waist by a leather belt, set with a shiny brass buckle.

"El Paso . . . ," she said thoughtfully as she sat down at the table with him. "How far from here to El Paso?" she asked.

"About six hours, Señorita. I also teach," he said with a smile. "I teach at one of the school districts in El Paso."

Carmelita felt the urge to stand up and kiss him, but on this night the anger, this newest of emotions for her, made her bolder than kisses.

"I need to get to El Paso, Enrique. You have no idea how timely your visit is to me," Carmelita said urgently.

Enrique laughed loudly, "Believe me, I pity anyone living around my cousins. With all due respect, they are the biggest pests I have ever known! They bother me all the time in El Paso, which is why I'm here. They send letters constantly, telling me how they're starving and how rich I must be in Los Estados Unidos. Of course, they constantly ask for one thing or another."

By this time Carmelita had forgotten her anger and was nodding her head in agreement, laughing at his accurate description of the Andrés family, and feeling united with him in a common cause against the unruly clan.

Without realizing it, Carmelita was talking and laughing with Enrique as if she had known him for years.

"If you'd like, Carmelita," he said, using her name for the first time, "you can come with me when I leave for El Paso this week. Would there be any problem in your leaving?"

"The problem would be in my staying!" she said, and they both laughed, understanding that she was leaving nothing behind her but trouble.

"Do you like mangos, Enrique?" Carmelita asked suddenly, holding up the half-eaten mango.

"I've always said they are the most excellent of fruits," he replied.

(OBRA

The rain falls on the rooftop in steady, slanting sheets. Cobra sits under the weather-worn back porch breathing in the watery mist. The darkness holds him fast.

A miniature searchlight appears as the back door is opened. The light's angular beam illuminates half of Cobra's body, the square slab of concrete floor, and two legs of the kitchen chair he's sitting on.

"It's your mother on the phone," says Silvia loudly. Her voice jars Cobra back to the house, the backyard, the chain link fence a few yards away.

"Did you call her?"

"Why should I? She knows. Everybody knows. So what's new?"

Cobra walks into the house, edging in past his wife.

"Here we go again," she sighs.

Picking up the phone, Cobra runs one hand over his fatigue jacket, brushing off invisible raindrops. His clothes feel drenched.

"I'm OK, Ma" he says into the receiver. He sticks the phone under his chin and lights a cigarette.

"Silvia's making a big deal out of nothing." He glares at his wife. "She's not going anywhere."

"You bet I am!" shouts Silvia. She walks up to Cobra and shoves her hand roughly into his shoulder. "Right now! I'm leaving now!"

"Nothing, Ma. Nothing's going on. She's nuts, that's all."

"I'm nuts? I'm no lunatic sitting out in the rain."

"Shut up. You'll wake up Jimmy."

"What do you care about Jimmy? You don't care about anybody but yourself!"

"No, Ma! Don't come over. Everything's OK. Damn these women!" Cobra hangs up the phone with a bang and crushes his cigarette in the ashtray.

"Run, why don't you!" yells Silvia. "Go back outside. Feel sorry for yourself. Catch pneumonia—what the hell do I care? I swear I'm packing tonight! Twenty years of this is more than enough."

Cobra watches his wife run past him.

"Silvia, wait a minute." He sees her disappear down the hallway. He runs after her into the bedroom just as she starts pulling clothes out of the dresser. Cobra takes hold of her arm roughly, keeping her from reaching for more.

"Let me go! I told you I'm sick of all this Vietnam shit! You tell me I don't understand—it's always I don't understand. What's there to understand? You went over there and it was kill or be killed, and you still can't get over it?"

Cobra releases his grip. "There's a lot more to it than that."

"Then tell me, Carlos. Tell me! I've been asking for twenty years."

Cobra's body trembles. He sits down on the bed and stares at his wife. Her disheveled hair clings to her face, and the top button of her flowered blouse is missing.

"For God's sake, Carlos, tell me!"

Cobra opens his mouth to speak, but the words won't go past his lips. A suffocating smell of decaying matter permeates the air. He shuffles his feet instinctively, feeling knee-deep puddles. He hated not knowing what lay below the murky surface. He would rather have thrown his M16 like a boomerang to the opposite bank, torn off his boots, and taken his chances at swimming.

"Secrecy is the key," the sergeant had told him. "We gotta beat these gooks at their own game." How? The enemy was everywhere all at once, disappearing and reappearing like phantoms.

Silvia breaks into his thoughts, "Don't get that look again. How do you think I've felt all these years? Do you care? Look at me." She frames her husband's face between her hands. "Carlos, look at me."

He stares at her briefly, stares deep into the brown eyes that he saw in his dreams. The same eyes he wanted to lose himself in when he stood like a statue in the pouring rain next to Alberto, his best buddy. The guys all called him Big Al, and his reputation for generosity and loyalty were unsurpassed. Cobra remembered Big Al's broad back moving ahead of him, muscles bulging under his army green. Cobra used Big Al's face and voice to measure his sanity. If he could still see and hear Big Al he knew where he was, who he was.

Cobra's cousin, Augustine, warned him over and over again before he was drafted. "Take my word for it—they're gonna empty the barrios and ghettos first. Then they're gonna look to the American apple-pie crowd when they need officers. Nosotros los vatos, we don't stand a chance. Ever hear of a Chicano who wasn't in artillery? But this is where all them moves I taught you will help. Don't forget all my lessons, scramble up the moves, confuse them. Kung fu all the way."

Augustine was a master of martial arts and gave Carlos the name Cobra. "You weave and attack just like a real cobra," he said as they practiced moves in the backyard. "You'll be dangerous someday, little vato, a true-blue cobra all the way." Augustine held his cousin's arm behind his back, and with one quick twist and twirl he flung the boy to the grassy lawn. "There, let that be a lesson on what can happen if you let your guard down."

"I let my guard down," mutters Cobra.

"You what?"

"Remember Big Al?"

"How could I forget? Every letter you wrote had some news about him. Why did you stop writing me, Carlos? Why didn't you answer my letters the last months you were there?"

"I couldn't. Something happened, and I couldn't do it. Couldn't explain it to you. Couldn't talk about anything to anybody."

"What did you want to say?" Silvia asks, enclosing her husband's hands in her own.

"Don't run, Carlos. You've run so long. I'm tired. I've been chasing you down, and I want to stop. We owe it to our grandchild—to Jimmy—and to our son. God, isn't it enough that Ben's locked up in prison? What will Jimmy remember about his own father? And Marci—look at her life. What did we do wrong with our daughter? Carlos, we have to start from the time you quit writing. This country doesn't deserve our lives."

"Big Al knew," says Cobra stiffly. "He knew he wasn't gonna make it. 'I got this feelin',' he told me. 'This feelin',' and he pointed to his heart. 'You're gonna make it, ese, and when you do, take this letter to my jefita in L.A.' He was so proud of his little old mother. Never knew his dad. He got mad when I told him how I squared off with my old man. I wasn't gonna let him beat up on my mom anymore. You remember don't you, Silvia? Tell me I wasn't too hard on him."

"You weren't. He did everything but break your mother's jaw. What do you expect? You were a kid standing up for your mom."

"But he called me before he died, and I never went to see him." Cobra's voice breaks. He slumps over on Silvia's shoulder.

"Carlos, your father was a bastard! You know it as well as I do."

"But listen to this, Silvia. Maybe I'm one too. I'm worse. I wasn't there for someone who stood by my side."

"Big Al?"

"He was always taking shit for me. What was he, my own guardian angel or something? Times I was high, times I didn't know what the hell I was doing, he was there. But when it was my turn, I didn't do the same."

"What didn't you do?"

Cobra sees the image of Big Al's face coming towards him, unrecognizable in the blurry light. He feels the pelting rain splash blood all over his jacket and hears the staccato beat of raindrops on his helmet. Split seconds before the bullet hit, he knew what he should have done.

"I froze."

Cobra looks past his wife at the retreating figure of the enemy. He sees the gun poised, pointing at Big Al, ready to blast. He has less than a split second advantage, but it's there, the time he needs, etched between him and the enemy's eyes.

Cobra lets out a wail. The howl of a wounded animal sounds from the pit of his stomach. His sobs open old wounds, pain that has never healed. Each sob brings one more stabbing accusation to the surface.

Silvia rocks her husband in her arms like she rocked Ben and Marci when they were babies, like she now rocks two-year-old Jimmy to sleep. Her body is a moving wall, warm and tender, sturdy and unresisting.

"Shhhh, listen to me, Babe. You were a kid. Carlos, you were eighteen. You saw a man. You didn't shoot. You couldn't control everything."

"But he shot my friend," gasps Cobra. "In the face. Silvia, he shot him in the face!"

"Forgive yourself."

"How?"

"Did you mean it? Did you want Big Al to die?"

"No, never!"

"Then your only mistake was not shooting fast enough. Break it down to what it was, Babe. You didn't kill Big Al, somebody else did. Don't kill yourself over what you should have done. Stop blaming the eighteen-year-old kid. He was scared. He wasn't such a big cobra after all."

Cobra shudders. "I've been sorry for so long and it still doesn't seem good enough."

"When will it be good enough for you, Carlos?" asks Silvia. Her throat aches. "When will the man I fell in love with come back to life again? I don't care what you did. I'm sorry for Big Al, but you were mine before you went to that stinking war, and I want you back. I've missed you for so long. Your funny smile, the way we ran out in the rain together. All your crazy pranks. God, Carlos, I need you to come back! The kids need you. Not even Big Al is mad at you. How could he be? He knew you better than you knew yourself."

Silvia hears her mother-in-law's voice in the kitchen. "Your mom's here," she says.

"Tell her I went to China. Tell her I'm dead."

Silvia walks out of the room and meets her mother-in-law before she gets to the bedroom door.

"How is he?"

"He went to China and died."

"What?"

"He's fine, Juanita. Really. Better than he's been in twenty years."

"Where's the baby?"

"Jimmy's asleep."

"I brought Augustine with me. Cobra always looked up to him," she says, adjusting her glasses.

Silvia makes out the outline of Augustine's beer belly as he stands by the kitchen sink.

"How's Cobra?" he asks.

"He's OK. It's been hard for him, Augustine. All these years, thinking about all the things he can't change."

"He was always too sensitive. Even after all the training I gave him. He was good but too touchy. He hated to see anybody in pain."

"Are you still leaving him?" asks Juanita. "I can't believe you would leave my son when he needs you so much."

"What about what I need?" asks Silvia impatiently. Her heart pounds in her throat. "What about what the kids need, Juanita? Should I just keep looking the other way?" She walks into the dining room.

Juanita follows. "You're blaming Cobra for all this?" She drops her purse then picks it up again. She puts her hands on her hips.

"I'm blaming nobody for nothing. Something happened in Vietnam. Something Carlos has to forgive himself for. It has to be done. Just like paying taxes and dying. He has to do it."

"He has to put it in God's hands," ascertains Juanita.

"First he has to *want* to put it in God's hands, and that has to come from him."

"Miguel should have been the one to go," says Juanita.

"That wimp? He can't even stand up to his own shadow! Don't tell me anything about Miguel. You know you protected him. Yes, admit it, you protected him, sending him to school, and making Carlos go to work."

Juanita takes two steps towards her daughter-in-law and waves her finger in Silvia's face. "You have the nerve to talk to me that way! I begged Cobra not to go. I told him to run. I wanted to hide him in Mexico. Not even the FBI could have found him!"

Silvia feels as if her hair is being pulled up from its roots. "You liar!" she shouts. "You know you chose Miguel and your husband. After all he did to you, you still stayed with him."

Silvia sees her mother-in-law's hand rise to strike her, but she doesn't move. She allows her to strike and feels the sting on her face, a flesh-and-blood whiplash.

"Ma, leave her alone!" shouts Cobra.

Juanita turns around to see her son behind her with Augustine at his side.

"Are you OK, Babe?" he asks Silvia.

"Yeah. She's not as strong as she looks."

"So you're taking her side now, are you? I might have known. Nunca, no never was I able to trust your father, and you're just like him."

"The hell he is!" yells Silvia. "He's nothing like the animal you married. He feels things. His heart bleeds. And he's no wimp like Miguel."

"Are you gonna stand there and let your wife insult me like this?"

"You better go," says Cobra to Augustine. "Take Ma back home now."

Juanita begins to cry, holding her hands up to her face.

"Ma, it's OK." Cobra walks towards her, putting out his arms to hold her.

"No, don't touch me. You have no respect for me, just like you didn't respect your father."

"Ma, how could I respect him? I never saw any good in him. Forgive me, but don't make me into the kind of man he was. Ma, don't you understand? I'm not him."

"Tía, let's go," says Augustine, already walking to the door.

"And stop calling him Cobra!" shouts Silvia as they walk out. "I hate that name. It doesn't fit him." The door closes with a bang.

"I didn't know you hated that name."

"I hate anything that comes between us."

He holds Silvia in his arms, kissing her and pressing his hand gently on the side of her face that sustained his mother's blow.

"How would you like to go outside and play tag?" he asks, smoothing back her hair.

"Carlos, it's raining."

"Of course! Remember? Come on, I'll race you!"

They dash out into the front yard and chase each other around the chinaberry tree until they are thoroughly drenched. They feel like kids again—laughing, holding each other in the rain.

ISABEL'S JUDGE

The first time Isabel saw a judge she was only eight years old. Her cousin, who had lived with them since his mother died and his father was sent to prison, stood before the fumbling old judge of the sixth district court. Isabel thought of her cousin as an older brother, older only in years, not in strength or maturity. He seemed to always be in need of protection, living in a house not his own and faced with the teasing and bullying of the other children. Isabel found herself worrying about him, especially when he went out into the barrio and she knew she wouldn't be around to defend him. She sometimes expected to hear that her cousin had been beaten to death, his skinny body broken in half.

Sitting in the hushed courtroom, Isabel leaned on her mother's ample arm. She could feel the tight fit of her mother's sleeve and the warm moistness of her arm through the thin material of her dress. She looked up at the ceiling fans, two of them rotating above her head, and her eyes followed the dome-shaped ceiling edged in wood trim.

Her cousin was brought in just as Isabel began tracing an imaginary line from one corner of the curved dome ceiling to the other to make a perfect X right over the place where she figured Títere—his real name was Flavio—would stand. Everyone knew him as "Títere" because people said he acted like a puppet dangling at the end of a string. He followed whoever was pulling his strings. His thin, flat body even looked like that of a puppet. The name was a perfect description of why Títere was facing the judge today.

"No mind of his own," Isabel's mother said, pointing to her head.

"Poor Títere," said Isabel's father, trying to sound compassionate. "He's a fool and will never amount to anything."

With these words Títere became even more of a puppet than Pinocchio had been, and worse still, he had no blue fairy to wave her magic wand over him and make him real.

The side door in the old courtroom, half of it a hazy glass, opened and in walked three prisoners chained together, each in bright orange coveralls. Títere was the last one and seemed to have the most difficulty walking, for the two ahead of him rattled the single chain this way and that as they walked.

Isabel jumped up and said, "Ma, there's Títere!" and her mother instantly grabbed her arm and sat her back down again. Títere raised his eyes from his rubber thongs and glimpsed Isabel in her pink polka-dotted dress, her ponytail clasped with a matching pink barrette.

Isabel never forgot the look on her cousin's face as long as she lived. His eyes resembled those of her cat, Gordo. Every time she caught Gordo on the bed, where he wasn't supposed to be, he looked at her half-alarmed, mild and expectant, waiting for the punishment to come, hoping it wouldn't come at all. Títere's eyes reflected another emotion; gratitude gleamed, nearly pushing tears to the surface.

As soon as they were seated, the sound of wood hitting wood echoed sharply in the courtroom, and an officer announced "All rise. The Honorable Theodore M. Buckley, judge of the Sixth District Court, presiding."

Isabel's heart pounded in her throat, and even her mother shuffled her feet nervously. The judge, in a black robe, sat between two flags on his high bench overlooking the half-empty courtroom. He felt around on the polished bench top like a blind man, searching for his glasses.

Upon finding them, he propped them midway up his nose. For several moments of silent suspense he read documents, seeming at times to pause and read a passage over again as if he couldn't quite make out what he was reading. For a few seconds Isabel thought he had fallen asleep; then in a quaking but loud voice he announced, "Flay-veeo Cabree-o, approach the bench."

Títere stole one more trapped glance at Isabel, then an officer unlocked the chain to release him. He walked, rubber thongs flapping, right to the spot where Isabel had drawn her imaginary X.

The judge looked at him, coughed, then looked at him again as if he couldn't believe what he was seeing.

"Have you anything to say for yourself before I sentence you?" he asked in a threatening voice.

"No," came the whispered reply from Títere.

"Look up at me!" ordered the judge as Títere continued to look down at his feet.

"Is your mother here?"

"No," came the far-away response.

"Well, where is she then?" boomed the judge's voice.

"At the cemetery," said Títere, clasping his hands behind his flat back. Without a pause the judge asked, "And where is your father?"

"In prison," said Títere, looking away from the judge and straight at one of the flags.

"Well, now, what have we here, a family reunion? Like

father, like son. You'll be seeing your old man very soon, if you can find him in there. They all look alike to me," said the judge, pushing his glasses up on his nose to get a closer look at Títere.

"There's not much of you, is there?

Títere didn't respond.

"Took advantage of the freedom of our great land, did you? Robbing liquor stores and running rampant with honest money others have worked for. Well, we'll see how far that gets you in the big house! For shaming your mother in her grave and following in your father's footsteps, I sentence you, Flay-veeo Cabree-o, to fifteen years in the state penitentiary."

When Isabel heard the harsh sentence, it seemed that she herself had been judged. This first courtroom scene never faded from her memory, in spite of the fact that there were to be many such encounters. Her own brother would be faced with a prison term, as would an assortment of cousins who would make their way to judges, linked on chains and led in by officers of the court to face sentencing for robberies, drug charges, and assaults.

On the night Isabel decides to run away from Gilberto, the only court scene she remembers clearly is the day Títere was sentenced to fifteen years. Isabel sits in a battered old armchair, her eyes closed with weariness, her body alert for every sound, every movement. The room's only light comes from a street lamp that shines through the window of her small apartment.

Opening her eyes, Isabel makes out the outline of two small bundles under a blanket where her two children are sleeping on a narrow bed. Isabel wonders where Títere is at this moment. She heard he had come out on good behavior after seven years, only to return within a year. After that the family counted him as one of the lost, one of those destined to live behind bars for the rest of his life. "It's better for him," her mother said. "At least he'll be fed. God knows he needs it."

"And who will feed me and my children?" Isabel wonders, feeling a maybe-I-was-wrong-after-all sensation creeping up from the pit of her stomach. So many regrets to talk over with the night. So many accusations she has to explain to the judge, who will order her to look at him then sentence her anyway. Sentence her for actions she didn't even know were crimes, although she knew they were wrong.

Yes, it was wrong to get pregnant before she married Gilberto. It was so wrong she never had the nerve to tell her parents but instead had deceived them into the temporary belief that she and Gilberto had planned to get married anyway, but now they had decided to do it more quickly. Passion couldn't wait. Everyone understood that. Then, when the truth made itself known—and how easily it made itself known—through Isabel's expanding middle, her mother lashed out at her for dragging the family's honor through the mud.

"What have I done wrong?" cried her mother almost every time she saw Isabel. "What have I done to deserve this?"

The severity of the sentence doubled for Isabel. Not only had she married Gilberto, a manipulator who saw himself at the center of his own universe, but she had obeyed him when he told her to quit school. One scholarship after another was offered to Isabel in recognition of her high grades and participation in school activities. She had learned something from facing all those courtrooms and judges. When you stand before a judge, you can expect the worst. So Isabel had taken it upon herself to always excel so that no judge would ever mispronounce her name and make her cower under his gaze.

When Gilberto threw Isabel's books all over the cracked linoleum floor, he yelled at her, "You and your big-time brains are going nowhere! You're gonna stay home and take care of this kid, and that's the end of it!"

Isabel glared at him, daring him to hit her. She had found out that to evade this judge she mustn't show fear, for he thrived on it. She had to replace fear with a show of fearlessness, even if she risked a slap on the face.

Isabel had to serve her parents' sentence in a different way. She remained for them a loving, docile daughter who, in spite of all her intelligence and looks, didn't have enough brains to choose something better than Gilberto or to prevent herself from getting pregnant before she got married.

"Quien le manda," said her Tía Beatrice, always ready to prosecute others while forgetting her own crimes. "She made her bed, now she'll have to lie in it." And with this she figured she had given her favorite niece her best piece of advice, for she also felt embarrassed for having believed in Isabel.

She had so much to pay back. So many people she had hurt, so many she had disappointed. Her sister Veronica told her, "I thought you of all people would be the one to make it out of this family, and now look at you."

She never considered that she had done the same thing five years earlier. She believed that Isabel should have been smarter and wiser, should have known better after seeing her go through all the pain.

When would Isabel learn her lesson? More explanations when she had to go to school and notify her teachers that she wouldn't be attending anymore. Shock and disbelief met her at every corner. One counselor said, "There can't be a good reason for this decision, Isabel. Do you realize all you will lose?" He shook his head in anger and frustration because he too had depended on her to show all the other girls from the barrio that they could make it. Education was the key, the open door. Now he would have to eat his own words and go back to pinning his hopes on one or two other girls who hadn't been swayed by a Gilberto just yet.

Staring into the dark room, Isabel's mind feels crowded, as if all the judges of her life are sitting together on the same bench, pointing crooked fingers at her while she stands under the big X, wearing a pair of thongs, looking down, looking aside, never at their faces. She's traveled so long, received so many sentences that she feels there aren't enough prisons in which she can carry out her punishment.

Isabel jumps up from her chair when she hears a sound at her apartment door. Someone is standing outside but not knocking.

Then she hears her sister's voice from behind the door. "Open up. It's me, Veronica."

Isabel opens the door cautiously. She sees her sister and a man standing in the shadows. "Don't be afraid; it's not Gilberto," says Veronica as she hugs Isabel. "Look who I brought with me."

Standing two heads taller than Veronica is a man of medium build wearing gray khaki pants and a white shirt. Isabel stares in disbelief, her hand over her open mouth, for there outlined behind her sister is Flavio, also known as Títere.

"No! I can't believe it," says Isabel in amazement. "And here I was remembering the time you went up before the judge." Before she says another word, her cousin wraps her in his arms, no longer bony, and encloses her in a giant abrazo.

"That was the first time," he says smiling broadly, "and I never forgot the way you looked at me when I walked into that courtroom. Your eyes told me you would have stood in my place." Títere brushes away tears that gather in his eyes and hugs Isabel again.

"What did you expect? You were so skinny and defenseless, I didn't even know if you would survive prison," says Isabel, her own tears falling.

"It wasn't easy, Cousin. No, not at all. And many times I had to fight for my life, but I always remembered that you would have done battle for me."

The three walk into the apartment and Isabel turns on a small lamp to be sure that what she is seeing is still real with the lights on. Títere approaches the sleeping children and tenderly pulls the blanket away to see them.

"Beautiful kids. What are their names?" he asks.

"Anna and Joshua."

"Sounds gabacho," says Títere laughing. "I've got two of my own, and a wife, and a job. Yes, what a surprise!"

Sitting in the same chair Isabel sat on just a few short moments ago, Títere tells her the story of his comings and goings in prisons until last year when he decided that enough was enough of judges and courtrooms and tasteless gabacho food.

"I knew I had to make a decision because no one could make it for me," he says, "There was a certain way of life that I had dreamed about, and that was the way I wanted to live. I wanted what other men had—a wife, kids, a chance at life—but instead I did the opposite—got tats, did drugs, left my wife and kids, and stole to stay alive."

"I didn't do that," says Isabel, "But I married Gilberto. You might say I had my own personal jailer."

"I heard. Veronica wrote and told me you had married

him. I never liked that vato. He thought he had every woman wrapped around his finger."

"I thought Títere should know," says Veronica to Isabel, "Both of you were always so close."

"Why didn't you write me?" asks Títere.

"I was embarrassed. I knew you'd be disappointed like all the rest."

"Me?" Títere asks increduously, "Now how could I, a common criminal, have anything to say to you?"

"I guess I wanted so much out of life, and it seemed I was giving it all up," answers Isabel.

"I guess judges come in all shapes and sizes," says Títere, "Sometimes they even look like us."

"I've got plans now," says Isabel, excitedly. "Real plans, more plans for the things I want to do."

"Hey, Cousin, looks like we both done our time, que no?"

"Yeah," says Isabel, thinking that she now has so many plans she wants to live out that she won't have time to present herself in court, much less sit behind the bench.

PABLO THE PENITENT

The sun disappeared behind the jagged ridge of moutains, sinking slowly in a glowing globe of color as Pablo watched from his position on the three-legged stool. It always surprised him to see how quickly the sun moved in the sky, leaving faint fingers of purple, orange, and red streaks that beckoned to the night. Even this was an illusion, considered Pablo, for everyone knew that the sun didn't move at all.

The daytime hues turned to shades of black and gray, and lengthening shadows took possession of the desert landscape. Already the short, barrel cactus looked like so many stones thrown in heaps by a giant ogre who had tired of using them in his slingshot. The tall saguaros, arms held up towards heaven, grasped the last threads of light, held them momentarily, then gave them up to the night. Darkness caught up to the desert, veiling it in complete obscurity.

Carefully observing the moon advance across the sky, Pablo felt a deep urge to howl at it. To howl out his loneliness, his madness, and the illogical, unreasonable passion that left him speechless and weak as a child when he thought of Rosa's eyes looking into his. The full moon that now loomed before him had to know that her eyes were the most beautiful things he had ever seen. The moon was supposed to understand love. Under its light, lovers found one another. This had always been so.

So deep in thought was Pablo that he didn't hear approaching footsteps on the sandy ground. The footsteps stopped as they turned the corner of the makeshift house made of old planks and a few bricks that grounded the tottering structure.

"Buenas noches, Pablo."

Without turning to look, Pablo answered, "It's no use, Hernando. You shouldn't have come out here. I told you before that I won't go back."

"Do you expect to live out here in this dump forever, then?" asked Hernando. "Are you crazy? Is that it? Because if it's only craziness, we can still do something about it."

Ignoring the remark, Pablo said, "Hernando, have you ever felt so low, so less than nothing that you felt like there wasn't anything good inside you, like you were already dead but still breathing?"

"Man, you talk crazy!" said Hernando. "I told you when you married Rosa that she would drive you out of your mind. Now look at you! Didn't I tell you that you can't love a woman like that? She'll cut you up into a thousand pieces. But no, you never listen to me."

"Does it matter to you at all that you've been unfaithful to your wife?" asked Pablo sharply. His eyes held on to the moon and the black canopy before him. "Just answer me. Does it matter to you?"

"All men are like that," said Hernando, walking closer to Pablo. His work boots left impressions in the soft sand. "It's no big deal. Women expect us to play around at times. As long as they don't really find out. My thing is to always deny. Deny, deny, deny. That's the key to freedom."

"You didn't answer my question," said Pablo. "I want to know if it matters to *you*, not to a lot of other men."

"I suppose it does at times," answered Hernando hesitantly. "At times I try to stay away from other women. Then before long there's another one just waiting for me. But it really means nothing to me, nothing at all. I love Angela."

"How can you say that?" asked Pablo, now looking up to search Hernando's face for the truth. "You love her, yet you don't mind chasing other women."

"Oh, you're all messed up because you really love Rosa. Is that it? I knew that woman had you by the balls!" exclaimed Hernando with a laugh.

At his words Pablo felt a sharp pain go straight through his heart. Rage assaulted him and he stood up, fists hardened at his sides. "Get out of here!" he yelled. "Get out before I make you eat those words!"

"Threats don't move me, compadre," shouted Hernando stepping back. "If it's gonna be me and you, then we'll see who the best man is after all."

Seeing Pablo's eyes shining with rage, Hernando for once knew he couldn't match the look of murder in Pablo's eyes nor the swift way Pablo lunged at him, every muscle taut and ready for action.

"Everybody's right—you have gone crazy!" Hernando yelled. Both men stood half-leaning into each other, fists clenched, eyes locked, and for a few tense seconds it seemed the desert would witness a fight to the death. Hernando sensed that if the fight started, it would not end until he was knocked out or dead. There was no one around who would come to his rescue, and he was sure that Pablo would win.

"Calm down, why don't you?" said Hernando, unclenching his fists, his voice dropped slightly. "I'm leaving. I never intended to stay. Just doing a favor for Rosa, checking up on you. It's not many men who decide to live out in the town dump."

"Don't ever mention Rosa's name again," hissed Pablo between clenched teeth. And he walked away into the night, leaving Hernando staring after his mute figure.

It didn't take long for everyone in town to hear what Hernando had to say about Pablo. He explained to everyone that Pablo really had gone crazy, and wouldn't listen to anyone. "It's true; he's out in the dump! He looks like garbage himself. His hair isn't combed, his beard is grown out, and he's covered in dirt and sweat from head to foot."

"And to think I helped raise him after his father died," said Tío Chencho.

"His poor wife, Rosa!" added Tío Chencho's wife. "Not to mention his little old mother. My goodness, she must be about eighty-five years old. How will they ever survive this embarrassment?"

The word was out. Pablo had gone totally mad and no one could talk any sense into him. Rosa heard it all and spent most of her time inside the house when she came home from working as a secretary for Don Tomás Aguilar, who owned his own accounting business. She might have gone to find her husband herself, but she thought of her own wounded heart and the many times she had begged him to turn away from his life of drinking and carousing, which to her mind was at the crux of their problems. Mixed in with her feelings of love for Pablo, Rosa sensed a deep loneliness and loss, for she knew Pablo had lived in the dump long before he had actually moved there.

"A beautiful woman like you shouldn't even have to think of a man such as Pablo," Don Tomás said to Rosa daily. "He hardly knows what he's lost. But never mind; I'm here at your service. You can depend on me even if the whole world abandons you."

Then he laid his fat, heavy hand on Rosa's shoulder in fatherly fashion and let it linger there for a few seconds more than he had ever permitted himself before Pablo went mad. His fingers pressed ever so slightly into Rosa's tender flesh, and he already had a familiar spot he loved to soothe.

Rosa always moved away from Don Tomás's heavy hand, hoping he would notice she didn't need his condolences. Not once had she shown Don Tomás any tears, and if her husband was crazy, she certainly didn't want to talk about it with him!

"Thank you, Don Tomás," Rosa said nicely, "but my problems with Pablo are my own. Someday he'll come to his senses." But Rosa didn't believe her words and only said them to protect herself from her lecherous boss.

Rosa found herself moving away from all men, just as she moved away from Don Tomás. It reminded her of all the times when, even as a child, a man's hot gaze on her made her face turn bright red, and she would look for ways to draw attention elsewhere. Now it seemed she had to do this all over again, beginning with Don Tomás and ending with Hernando, for even he now played the role of consoling best friend, coming every day to check up on her to make sure she and the kids had food to eat, and money to pay the bills.

When he dropped by after work, his breath smelling of his last beer, she opened the door and left him standing out on the porch, assuring him things were fine. His questions got more personal and his conversations more lengthy. What kind of perfume did she like? Just asking. Only curious. Then the following day Rosa received a small bottle of perfume from the hand of Hernando, who asked her to wear it and think of him.

"Have you forgotten that Pablo's still alive?" she asked him.

"Half a man, I would say," answered Hernando. His eyes traveled smoothly over Rosa's splendid, translucent face with lips so round and full it seemed to Hernando that Pablo could never appreciate their luscious merits like he could.

The night Hernando refused to fight Pablo because he knew he would be beaten up was the same night Pablo wrapped himself up, although the weather was warm, and looked straight up into the moon, challenging its solemn, fierce light to bring sanity back to him instead of taking away the little he still clung to. Never had he felt as wild and savage as he did the night his heart told him he could have murdered Hernando and not regretted a second of the bloody battle.

In the moonlight his mind played not a single trick on him and he remembered Hernando's face as it was on the day he and Rosa were married. And they knew, he and the moon, that the secret glances he thought he saw Hernando give Rosa were true and not a part of his imagination or jealousy for Rosa.

"I've been such a fool!" he shouted, arguing with himself between sobs. Pablo stood beneath the moon and wept like a man does when he no longer cares that he's a man and shouldn't weep.

He cried for all the times he had listened to Hernando's drunken suggestions. "No one will know. We'll be right back. Rosa will always be there for you." Then he was led like a man sleepwalking right into the arms of one more woman at a bar or dance or party. It always seemed there was one woman left over, one without a partner, and that's where Pablo came in. He shared Hernando's fun. "One for you, one for me. We're friends after all, compadre. I have never been one to let myself be ruled by a woman, heh, compadre."

The drunker they got, the closer they got, until they weren't just compadres, they became hermanos united in defying death and hours of toil in the hot sun.

Streaks of fresh tears ran down Pablo's dirt-caked face as the moon rose higher in the sky, free and crystal clear. It appeared so close, Pablo saw boulders on its mountain tops and dried rivers forming wavy lines on its surface. And he saw again, like he did every night, the face of the small boy who had walked innocently into his mother's room one night, rubbing his sleepy eyes, barefoot, in his underwear, looking for his parents' bed to sleep in.

"Papa?" came the voice in the dark, and Pablo turned from his night of drunken lovemaking to see the tiny, white face of a child looking in perfect innocence for the face of his father to appear before him. Instead he had seen Pablo and let out a shriek of fear that sent Pablo scrambling to his feet in spite of his half-drunken condition. The woman he was sleeping with, also half-drunk, simply called to the child to get out, to leave, that his father wasn't in bed with her.

As Pablo fumbled with his clothes in the dark, he saw the child's face once again, and its expression of anger, hatred, and helpless disbelief that the face he saw before him in the dark was not his father's. Then the child was gone. Pablo heard muffled sobs in one corner of the house as he left that night. It was the darkness of night that made his escape possible, and it was the darkness within that made his escape necessary in the first place.

The night called out to him, hissing and mocking, "You are like me. You are dark. You do not deserve to live in the light." Night's cold, uncaring lips pressed at Pablo's ear. And Pablo ran. He ran into the eyes of shame and terror that he had recognized in the face of the child, in the distorted face of innocence he had seen in the dark. Unable to find relief that first night, Pablo had run to the edge of the small town to the dump, the place where everyone sent that which was no longer of any use to anyone. And the dump received him as one of its own, broken, tattered, unable to stand except on one leg.

Pablo stayed one night, then he couldn't go back. What would he say to Rosa? To the holy sacredness in her eyes, so like the child's, looking deeply into his own. How could he touch her skin again? Skin so smooth it felt like silk under his fingers. What could he tell her about his shame, the child's face, and the shriek that sent the gunshot wound into his soul, which was bleeding still?

So Pablo stayed. And on this night, three weeks to the day, as he and the moon shared the sparse desert scene, Pablo noticed the reflection of light from an object that resembled his mother's sliver platter at home, the one she used when she graciously served the family's meal of spicy beef, fish, or chicken on a bed of rice and beans. He reached for the platter, which was partly buried in the sand, lifted it up to the moon, tears blurring his sight.

One side of the platter was scorched as if someone had left it lying on top of the stove. The rest of the platter was tarnished, the engraved scrolls and flowers with pointed leaves barely visible. Pablo lifted the silver platter up to his face and caught his distorted reflection.

There he was, his beard overgrown from days of madness, his eyes red and swollen from weeping. He noticed that his face was drawn, weight loss compounding his deathly appearance. But it was him. He still recognized himself, which was a sign to him that he hadn't gone totally mad. And he still knew he was Rosa's husband, her lover, her man.

He rubbed the silver platter over and over again on his pants legs, rubbing off the tarnish until the side of the platter that wasn't burned reflected more and more of himself. Clearer and clearer the picture became until the scorched side of the platter no longer mattered. Pablo raised the platter up to the moonlight, and it gleamed where he had rubbed off the tarnish. His face shone in the perfect light.

PENGUIN'S MOTHER

As far as anybody knew, Penguin's mother had never committed a mortal sin. She went to church faithfully every Sunday. Her dark hair hung in glossy waves down her back, and her simple dress, caught at the waist by a faded black belt, showed her trim, shapely figure. She commanded admiring looks from the men, and suspicious glances from the women.

"I've never been one to fool around. God is everywhere," she told her neighbor Esperanza. "Just because that worthless run-around of mine took off with another woman is no reason for me to go crazy."

The bitter herbs life served Penguin's mother eventually made her forget she had ever tasted anything sweet. Her huge, tragic eyes found fault with everything. And faults were easy to find in the dismal housing project where she lived with her children. Bleak yellowed lawns, sagging rooftops, and broken windows proclaimed more than poverty. There was hopelessness in the air, thick as the locusts buzzing away in the trees.

"You're not to open the door to anyone," she told her children every evening as she left for work at the meat packing company. "Do you understand?" Six-year-old Penguin smiled, showing one tooth already missing in the front.

Katrina, already in the seventh grade, half listened with

one ear glued to the phone receiver. She played mom to Penguin because she was older than he was and knew better. It was understood that Katrina would help Penguin with all his first-grade work while she struggled alone with the demands of homework from the junior high. Besides the homework, dinner had to be served at the kitchen table that sprouted a concrete leg. One wooden leg had cracked beyond repair, and Penguin's mother solved the problem by creating a new leg. She supported the warped table top on two concrete blocks stacked in the space vacated by the deformed limb.

The rest of the crowded apartment showed as much order and cleanliness as time and money allowed. Cheap prints from the Goodwill store hung on the walls, and a calendar from St. Isidro's church took up space next to the refrigerator. Important saints' days were noted by a star drawn in blue ink, and birthdays were colored in with a crayon. The living room and kitchen windows boasted handmade curtains that Penguin's mother had sewn from material found at a rummage sale. The bedroom windows were covered by pull-down shades, and nothing else.

Every morning Penguin's mother walked her two children to the school-bus stop, standing back while they waited with other children for the seven o'clock bus. Looking at her son, she silently prayed that he would gain strength in his legs and not have to wear the braces the doctor had suggested.

The way his feet turned outward made him walk like a penguin, which was how he got his nickname. Try as she would, Penguin's mother couldn't make the children stop calling him by his nickname. Then again, she didn't like his real name either. Everytime she heard the name Roberto it sent a message of hatred from her head to her toes. It wasn't Penguin's fault that his father was a run-around chasing women wherever he went. It was even known that a woman in the Bahamas had borne Roberto's child, and he had never even visited the Bahamas!

On the morning before Thanksgiving, Penguin's mother returned home after watching her children board the school bus. She hugged her threadbare sweater around herself, rubbing the backs of her arms briskly with her hands for warmth. She reflected that Penguin and Katrina needed coats for the winter and planned to ask the social worker at school for help. Walking into the apartment, she paused briefly to stand before the wall heater, first with her back to its hot slats, then facing it. She always turned the oven on "low" to help heat up the kitchen, but no matter how hard she tried, the apartment was still cold, because the plastered walls stored the chilly night air like the inside of a freezer.

Penguin's mother drank her usual cup of coffee as if in a trance. She had returned home from work at 2:00 A.M. and had only slept three hours. She felt as though she were walking under water. Extreme fatigue caused her to feel euphoric and detached from herself. She looked around at the kitchen and began to plan one more way to get rid of the roaches, spying a couple of big ones crawling out of the garbage pail.

Sitting at the table, she used a nail file to dig out dried blood that collected under her nails, then paused to sniff the rotten smell of blood mixed with microscopic pieces of animal flesh that clung to her hands. She wondered why she paused to smell such a foul stench but did it anyway. Then she washed her hands with the detergent she used for the dishes and smelled her hands again, checking for any traces of the meat that she handled at the packing company.

The turkey given to her by the Salvation Army was out

on the kitchen counter, and she mentally went over the entire Thanksgiving dinner to be sure she had everything she needed. It was lucky for her that rich people felt so generous during the holiday season, or they would have nothing to eat at all!

While making her son's bed that morning, Penguin's mother said a short prayer for him, asking God to strengthen his deformed legs. She massaged his fragile legs daily with olive oil, hoping they would become flexible, bending at the knees like the legs of normal boys and girls. Was it something she had eaten during her pregnancy? Had Margarita, her nosy neighbor, put the evil eye on him? Had it passed down through her family? No, never that! They were all known for sturdy limbs, excellent posture, and athletic ability. It had to be from Roberto's side. His family certainly had its share of weirdos, some of them doing time in prison.

How she had managed to marry into such a despicable family astounded Penguin's mother every day. Her dreams of becoming a nurse had evaporated into thin air when Roberto came into her life, promising her that she would never have to work again. "Too beautiful to work," he had said. "Stay home and be my movie star." She stayed home a total of three months before she got pregnant with Katrina. It was then that Roberto started dating other women as if she had only been one of his girlfriends. Instead of running back to sanity, to her parents' house, Penguin's mother stayed, investigating ways to win back her husband, which included having a brawl in a neighborhood tavern.

Once her anger had been unleashed, she not only beat up the woman she caught with her husband but had fought her way out of the tavern, hitting both men and women as she went. Thinking of this, Penguin's mother made the sign of the cross over herself, asking God to forgive her for such violence and assuring Him it wouldn't happen again. After blessing herself, she smiled at the thought of the victory she had won at the tavern, the pain held inside her so long finally smashing into people's faces, and giving her the strength of a bull. The force of such violence lingered within her, making her laugh, cry, and shake at the same time.

While she was mopping the floor with disinfectant Penguin's mother heard a knock at the door. This surprised her. She expected that everyone else in the projects would be just as busy as she was.

"Is it you, Esperanza? Come in, why don't you?"

"It's not Esperanza," answered a man's voice.

For a second Penguin's mother thought it was the voice of Roberto, and she looked around for something to hit him with but could find nothing hard enough to penetrate his thick skull. In the next instant she was straightening her hair, smoothing down her T-shirt over her ample breasts, and mentally recording that she was on her period, just in case.

Opening the door, Penguin's mother saw an imitation of Roberto. The man had the same wavy dark hair, moustache, and crinkly brown eyes that had made her forget her career and believe she was a movie star. She shivered, and her teeth started clattering even before he opened his mouth to speak.

"I'm Roberto's cousin. Don't you remember me? I'm Marco. Remember Teresa? She was my wife, the one Roberto was chasing at Susanna's wedding. I guess he caught up with her, after all!" At this he laughed and his breath made a smudge in the cold air.

"Teresa? What happened to her?" asked Penguin's mother.

"Who knows? I haven't seen her in five years. I've had a little business to take care of, you know, in the big house, but it's all over now."

Penguin's mother planted her bare feet even more firmly on the cold linoleum floor. She held the door half open and leaned her head sideways, which was the way she studied people she didn't trust. Marco had already taken in everything there was to know about her. Her hunger cried out to him, her need for a man's voice at her ear and a man's hands running up and down her body. And what a body! Time to collect from Roberto.

Not knowing what else to do, Penguin's mother opened the door all the way and asked him to come in out of the cold.

"Sorry for all the mess," she said, "but I'm getting ready for tomorrow."

"No problem," Marco said. "I can give you a helping hand, if you don't mind. I know how to cook a dinner fit for a king!"

He immediately took off his shoes so as not to leave skid marks on the wet floor and started moving furniture around so Penguin's mother could mop more comfortably into corners that she would have otherwise missed. Still euphoric from the weariness of not sleeping, Penguin's mother asked no further questions, and Marco moved in rhythm with her, standing close by when she bent down low to drag the wet mop under the couch. He even insisted on mopping the bathroom, and when he was finished he wrung out the mop in the pail and threw the dirty water out in the alley. Then he shook out the mop and slung it over the clothesline to dry.

It was then that Esperanza saw him as she glanced out her kitchen window. Her heart raced with fear, thinking it was Roberto. She ran to the phone to call Penguin's mother to ask if she should call the police.

"No," said Penguin's mother, "it's not Roberto. No, of course, there's no problem. He'll only be here a few hours. It's one of Roberto's close cousins, like a brother to him," she added nervously, thinking that the next call Esperanza would make would be to Corina, and then everyone in the projects would know.

Marco had already served himself a cup of coffee and was sitting at the kitchen table watching Penguin's mother on the phone. His eyes traveled down the length of her body, taking in her creamy, light skin and the queenly way her hair fell in huge waves around her shoulders. He noticed the sturdy shape of her buttocks under her stretch pants and the sensuous way she rubbed one bare foot against her leg as she talked on the phone. The profile of her breasts made his skin tingle with excitement.

"Well, what shall we do next?" Marco asked casually as Penguin's mother sat down at the table. "Shall we start on the salads, pies, or dressing?"

"Nothing right now," answered Penguin's mother sleepily. "I'll do everything later tonight. What I need to do right now is sleep. I came in at two this morning." Suddenly, it seemed to Penguin's mother that she hadn't slept in years. Just looking at Marco made her long to curl up in bed and go to sleep.

"Oh, I understand perfectly," said Marco, resting his hand on hers. "Again, if you don't mind, I'll just watch a little TV. It would be fun to see Penguin and Katrina again. I saw Penguin when he was barely born. And Katrina? She must be a beautiful girl by now."

The thought came to Penguin's mother that she should ask him to leave now. Yes, NOW! Out into the freezing morning, away, run away with the woman from the

Bahamas. She felt confused. She had forgotten, momentarily, that he wasn't Roberto. Of course, she thought with a yawn, he wasn't Roberto. He could stay. The kids would be glad to see him. She wanted only to get away from Marco's hot, heavy hand over hers and the scent of his body rising up over their coffee cups.

Penguin's mother closed the door of her bedroom and slipped under her warm blankets without taking off her clothing. She glanced at her bureau, where there was a veladora with a picture of the Sacred Heart on it. She made the sign of the cross over herself, asking God to protect her from evil. The candle's glow made a soft light in the darkened room.

Halfway through one of her dreams, Penguin's mother felt the touch of someone's hand on her face. Drowsily, she told Penguin to get ready for school, but the touch wouldn't go away. She opened her eyes and saw Roberto bending over her, kissing her lightly on her lips and forehead. His kisses felt good but tasted salty, not sweet. She enveloped him in her arms and moved over just a bit to let him lie next to her, then he rolled onto her as if he had never had other lovers, only her. Closing her eyes tightly so as not to look at the picture of the Sacred Heart, Penguin's mother felt her clothes falling off her body and her heart pounding in her head as the energy of lovemaking took over her body. It began like a tidal wave that burst forth from her and rushed into her ears. Wave after wave came and went until she was spent. Then she fell asleep like a baby.

At 2:00 in the afternoon the alarm clock rang. It was time to pick up the kids at the bus stop. Penguin's mother moved to get up and saw that Marco lay next to her, naked, snuggled up to her bare back. She jumped up and stood before him, her hair falling like a dark halo around her face.

He reached over and put his hand on her thigh. She looked at him in horror, her hand over her mouth.

"What's wrong?" he asked. "Isn't it natural for men and women to get together? You know you wanted it. Don't tell me you didn't."

"Get out!"she yelled. "Get your ass off my bed and get out!"

"Already?" Marco asked smiling. He lay his head back on his arms. "What's wrong? Don't you like what you see?"

By this time Penguin's mother had her clothes back on and was rushing out of the room.

"What are you gonna do?" asked Marco. "Are you calling the cops?" His voice reached her in the kitchen. "What are you gonna say to them when they ask you how I got in?" he shouted.

"I want you out of this house before I get back with the kids!" she yelled back at him.

By the time she came back with Penguin and Katrina, Marco was out of the house.He was sitting on the slab of concrete outside the front door.

"Hey, kids!" he said cheerfully. "Remember me, your old Uncle Marco?" Penguin and Katrina looked at him, their eyes widening. They looked at their mother and saw her gaze drop. She looked away from Marco and said, "He's your father's cousin, and he was just leaving."

Marco picked up Penguin in his muscular arms and swung him around in a circle. "How can I leave? We've just started having fun!" He held onto Katrina's hand and twirled her like a ballerina. "What a gorgeous girl you are! A movie star!" he said laughing.

Both children were charmed by the attention Marco gave them and happily hung onto him as they walked into the apartment together. That was how Marco got back into the apartment and got to stay for Thanksgiving dinner, Christmas, and New Year's. Every night he slept on the couch. And early in the morning when Penguin's mother came home from work, he slept in her bed, changing to the couch before the kids got up. Sometimes he didn't make it to the couch on time, and the kids pretended they hadn't seen he wasn't there.

Esperanza, Corina, and the rest of the neighbors didn't come over the whole holiday season because they didn't know how to approach Penguin's mother now that she had decided to take in a man. No one called her on the phone, and she didn't call anyone, either. What would she say? The kids like him. He looks like their father. Yes, of course, he sleeps on the couch. None of your business if anything else is going on.

Penguin's mother quit going to mass on Sundays and snuffed out the candle with the picture of the Sacred Heart. When she and Marco met, they met in the dark, and she didn't question if he was Roberto anymore. It stopped mattering to her—until the day after New Year's.

On that afternoon, Penguin snuggled up to his mother as she sat on the couch. Marco had gone out to the unemployment office to get his check. Penguin's mother knew that Marco would probably spend most of it on drinks and gambling before he got back home.

"Mama, my back hurts," Penguin whispered.

"Where?" she asked, and Penguin placed his hands low on his back.

"Lie down," she said. "Let me rub you with olive oil."

As Penguin's mother rubbed her son's bony back with olive oil, she noticed bruises on his buttocks and down his thighs.

"Did you get hurt, my baby?" she asked. Penguin didn't answer.

"Penguin, I'm asking you something," she said, her voice raising in pitch. "How did you get hurt?"

"I'm not supposed to tell, but Uncle Marco did that, because he plays games with me."

"What kinds of games?" asked his mother. She felt her mouth go dry. Her hands began to tremble.

"He told me not to tell you because you would get mad and would make him go away. You won't will you?" he asked. He glanced back at her, and his little body writhed in pain from the movement. Penguin's mother looked down at her son's bruised body and knew that the pain he suffered had been masked by his deformed limbs, making it difficult for her to notice any changes.

"Don't worry about what will happen to him, my darling," she answered. Her voice sounded disconnected to her, an empty sound her throat had just made. She dressed Penguin warmly and phoned Esperanza.

"Can I take Penguin and Katrina over to your place for a few hours? There's something I need to take care of."

"Is anything wrong?" asked Esperanza, flattered that her friend had even taken the time to dial her number.

"I'll tell you about it later," Penguin's mother answered flatly.

When Marco came home that night, he noticed that the lights on the Christmas tree weren't on and the apartment was pitch black. He switched on the light and saw no one in the living room or kitchen.

"I'm in here," called Penguin's mother from the bedroom.

"Just like all the other bitches I've ever had," muttered Marco to himself. "Once they open their legs to you, there's no closing them."

He staggered a bit walking down the hall and opened the door of the bedroom. The veladora was glowing in the dark, its circle of light reflecting off the ceiling. Penguin's mother sat in the middle of the bed, dressed in an old robe. She looked like a Buddha, with her hands folded in front of her and her legs crossed.

"A game?" asked Marco. "Now, you're talking! I love games!" He half-fell on the bed next to her, playfully putting his hand on the buttons of her robe.

"I'm sure you like games. Very sure," said Penguin's mother through clenched teeth. "Especially with little boys!" Marco sat up and glared at her in anger. He lifted his hand to slap her, but his hand never made it to her face. Penguin's mother took out the knife Marco had used to carve the turkey from underneath her robe and stuck it deep into his throat. She put all the pain of his betrayal in the force of the blow. It didn't alarm her when she saw bright red blood spurt all over her. She saw the butchering of animals at the packing company every night. She pulled out the knife and watched Marco struggle, gagging on his own blood, and finally she saw him drop to the floor.

Penguin's mother felt as powerful as she had felt that day in the tavern, as strong as a bull. Her feelings swept over her chaotically, rushing at her from every cell in her body. She laughed and cried, and her body shook in spasms. She ran to the bathroom and took a shower, dressing herself without turning on the lights. She washed off the knife, just like she did after she cut up meat at work. Then she blew out the candle, her tears reflecting the last sparkle of light.

When she returned to Esperanza's house, the children were already asleep.

"My God! What's wrong!" cried Esperanza. "You look like a ghost!"

"Esperanza, will you do me a favor?" asked Penguin's mother casually. "Call the cops. Tell them there's a dead animal in my bedroom and would they please come and pick it up."

That night Penguin's mother was taken away. She spent the night in jail laughing, crying, and shaking at the same time until all the trapped, ugly feelings in her life were released. One year later she was set free, because the judge said she was crazy when she stuck the knife into Marco. The apartment was eventually rented to a couple from China who couldn't speak a word of English and didn't understand why nobody else wanted to rent the apartment vacated by Penguin's mother.

DOÑA DOLORES

On a beautiful starlit night right before Margarita Estrella's birth, her mother reported to her husband that she had watched a shooting star whiz across the sky and disappear in a blast of sheer white light just behind the mountain's curving slope. It was then that she decided to name the child she carried "Estrella" in honor of the shooting star that had so graciously allowed itself to be seen. The baby was thus christened Margarita Estrella, the first name in honor of her mother's favorite flower, the daisy.

Growing up in the mansion her family owned in the heart of Mexico City, Margarita Estrella was surrounded by fine old houses, some with Mexican flags draped over the balconies, and landscaped lawns manicured to perfection. An array of beautiful flower gardens adorned the sloping lawns, and expensive automobiles gleamed in the sun behind wrought-iron gates. Many said she lived a life millions only dreamed existed.

Margarita Estrella was truly a star, even from birth. She grew up the eldest in a family of three children, watched over and cared for by servants who tended to her every need, afraid that any sneeze or cough might herald an unknown illness. Her dresses were tailor-made by a local seamstress, who worked out unique designs for each member of the family in her tiny shop that over the years expanded to a thriving enterprise with the money she made off the rich and mighty.

Margarita Estrella's life did not want for luxury and comfort, which is why those who lived around her became disappointed as she changed over the years into a woman filled with sorrow and pain. "Doña Dolores," everyone called her. "All she does is complain and complain."

How dare she be unhappy, protested the sophisticated women who buzzed around her life, spying on her, envious of her perfect body and queenly air. They gloated over her jewelry when they saw her at important city functions, picking out a necklace, bracelet, earrings, or ring that they liked the most. They discussed which fur wrap or handmade lace shawl she would wear for high society events when the weather was cool. And they wondered what went on in her head, since she took no one as confidante.

Her marriage to Eduardo Montoya had made enough news to last for a year of gossip at least. No one would ever forget the white doves released into a perfect noonday sky after the couple exchanged wedding vows. Then came the conjectures about the couple's ability to stay together and remain faithful—or rather to maintain an air of loving distraction and at all costs live a discreet life that would not involve their family in scandals.

The change in personality from Margarita Estrella to Doña Dolores defied public analysis. There had been a time when the marvelous couple had been invited to one social gathering after another, and they had appeared impeccably dressed, Margarita Estrella ever a star, her arm linked with that of her tall, stately husband, her smile outshining her jewels in radiance.

Envy crowded into the hearts of the women and men who greeted them with civility and respect, for to show less than deference to the beautiful and powerful couple was sheer folly. Eduardo Montoya's family laid claim to vast acres of land that was passed on from one generation of his family to another in spite of civil wars and the rise and fall of political leaders. Business interests both in Mexico and abroad gave his family name fame and prestige. Still, the truth was that Margarita Estrella became sadder and more distant with each new year.

Some blamed her firstborn for her troubles. "He broke his mother's heart with his insane ways," said one woman to another as she watched Margarita Estrella at a distant table in a plush café. "Why, I recall when Doña Dolores had little Eduardo. She was so happy. He was her whole world."

"Unfortunate what happened to him," replied the other woman as she daintily pierced the last morsel of cream puff with her fork.

"How can a mother ever get over such a thing?"

Both women were right in analyzing the relationship between mother and son as one of supreme importance in the life of Margarita Estrella. Her firstborn son, hardheaded and independent since birth, meant everything to her. When her husband was gone for long periods on business trips, she and her son spent countless hours together, often going to museums, visiting ancient ruins, or attending new exhibitions that the great city offered. At these times Margarita Estrella saw the world through the eyes of a child, and it was fresh and beautiful, a story to tell that had never been told before.

Her son, however, had one interest that caused Margarita Estrella constant worry and many tears. Little Eduardo loved heights and climbing, and most of all he wanted to learn how to fly. In spite of the constant care he received, he fell off rooftops and ladders in his attempts to reach the sky. Each time he fell, his mother gathered him in her arms, tending to his wounds herself, at times not even notifying her husband, who would suggest that perhaps his son should be sent to the boy's academy instead of receiving private tutoring at home. As he grew older, the younger Eduardo even wanted to give himself to the trade of window-washer for the high-rise office buildings that lifted their heads above the hustle and bustle of the city so that in this way he would truly be "in the sky".

"Mi hijo, forget your foolish plans and listen to your father. You'll be heir of all we have and will be a very important man someday," Margarita Estrella said to her son. Then she winced inwardly to think of her lively son becoming a caricature of her husband, distant and cold. Yet she had to inspire respect, otherwise her son might end up with no inheritance at all, the brunt of one of her husband's decisions to "teach him a lesson."

"Don't worry, Mama," the younger Eduardo answered." Someday I'll surprise my father and do exactly as he says!" Then he laughed and his mother laughed with him, resolving to scold him with more determination the next time.

The younger Eduardo decided he wanted to train as a pilot and receive his license before he reached the age of eighteen. There was no one to stop him once his decision was made, and certainly his father couldn't suggest that a scandal would ensue from the matter and that blackmail would follow.

The elder Eduardo was ever on the lookout for anything that might reflect a scandal on his family and possibly invite a blackmailer to threaten them with the knowledge of some shameful secret that could only be hushed by a good quantity of money or by favors that spelled further disaster. He was a master of discretion, conducting his affairs, both in business and in his social life, with the greatest of care.

It wasn't long after the younger Eduardo started flying that his enthusiasm for the sport got the best of him and claimed his life. Flying for long hours, he often forgot to look at his fuel gauge and many times landed on open fields or close to any available airport in search of fuel to continue his trip. It was discovered while investigating the crash that cost him his life that the plane had run out of fuel. The young man had zigzagged from the sky, landing on the backs of unsuspecting sheep grazing in an open pasture. The news reached Margarita Estrella just as she was coming back with her two younger children from a sporting event. She maintained her cool exterior composure and simply stated, "He's probably hiding in the bushes nearby and will come back as soon as his latest adventure is over."

Even the knowledge that her son's body was found did nothing to convince her of his death. "More than likely it's someone who was with him on the plane," she said to whoever would listen.

At her son's velorio, Margarita Estrella looked every bit Doña Dolores, although she continued to say that the remains were not those of her son and that perhaps he would soon be found living with an Indian family in the wild mountain country. She attended her son's funeral in body but with eyes that were blank, as if the pupils had no light left to reflect.

Her husband gave up on trying to convince her of reality and instead allowed her to continue her fantasy about their son if that would relieve her mind of its burden. However, the burden, not dealt with, became a part of the personality of Margarita Estrella, robbing her of her radiant smile and of the pleasure and newness that her son had always given her.

Margarita Estrella did not confide in others because her husband told her, "Be cautious. We don't want to arm our enemies and open ourselves up to blackmail." She wondered what could be used against her, since her life was so publicly lived she scarcely had private moments of her own.

She trained herself to look the other way when her husband's eyes caught a certain attractive young woman's gaze and she saw a small, hidden something exchanged between them. She found tickets to operas and plays in the pockets of her husband's most expensive jackets. She didn't remember being with him at these functions, but someone had been there. A business associate? Of course, he had so many business deals to close and many important people to entertain. Her mind didn't allow her to accept anything more. In the days when she still had her son, it wouldn't have mattered how many tickets she found in her husband's jackets. The need for her husband was filled up by the need for her son, until the day her son fell from the sky.

"Tragic that she can't get over that accident," said a woman to her friend as they watched Margarita Estrella one night in the lobby of El Teatro Magnífico. "Can you imagine—a closet full of clothes, and all she wears is black!"

Margarita Estrella was standing at her husband's side, apart and distant, not even pretending to listen to what others had to say. One gloved hand hung limply at her side, and the black dress she wore sagged at the shoulders, showing the severe weight loss everyone was used to by now.

"Does she ever hear from her daughter?" asked another inquisitive bystander, joining the other two women in the lobby.

"The last I heard, Anita was living in Oregon, in Los

Estados Unidos. They say it rains there all the time, and if it were me I wouldn't last there one minute."

Common knowledge was that Anita, the splendid-looking daughter of the illustrious couple, had fallen in love with an American student at the University of Mexico and had left with him to live in the United States without even asking her father's permission. Her American hero turned out to be nothing more than a dishwasher who traveled about the world by his wits.

Upon meeting the beautiful and wealthy Anita, he had assumed that his financial troubles were over and hadn't understood her father's uncompromising stance on disobedience and his unswerving vigilance for blackmailers. Alone with the spoiled young woman, he soon found out that he would have to keep at least three jobs going to please her, as no help was coming from her father.

"What about Xavier? I hear he lives right here in Mexico City and has established his own business," said the first woman to the other two. "Is he a comfort to her?"

To mention Xavier's name to Margarita Estrella made her eyes light up with the thought of her grandchildren, whom she adored. Just as quickly the light in her eyes died out, for the reality was that she hardly saw her grandchildren at all. Her daughter-in-law said she spoiled them too much, and she was bound and determined to bring them up to learn the benefits of hard work and not depend on their bloodline for security. She had new thoughts, new ways that demanded that each of her children make their own way in the world. Margarita Estrella, unwilling to suffer another loss, reasoned that her grandchildren were being well cared for by her son and his wife, and her pleading to see them, to hold their small, fragrant bodies safe in her arms was now a thing of the past.

Margarita Estrella's change from lively and joyous to sad

and dreary became more clearly defined as the years unraveled. If she spoke at all, she complained of stomachaches, pains in her chest, and headaches that wouldn't go away. One famous doctor after another was called in to examine her and analyze the many tests given to her, with no results except the declaration that she needed bed rest, tranquility, and peace.

This in itself was what her husband hoped to hear to avoid scandal. He didn't want a diagnosis of a real illness or a mental disorder that would set people to pointing fingers and assuming the Montoyas were less than rich and powerful, beautiful and healthy. Not once did he hold Margarita Estrella for longer than two minutes in the cordial embrace he had developed just for her. His happiness was complete when one of her many illnesses kept her in bed, and he had to find one of his business associates, one of the many vivacious young women that decorated his offices, to accompany him to social events.

"Poor Doña Dolores, ill in bed again. Hope she's better tomorrow," reflected one of his favorite associates to another. They giggled together and exchanged makeup in the ladies' room of the most expensive restaurant in La Plaza Central. In the dining room waiting impatiently for one of them sat Eduardo Montoya sipping champagne at a table reserved for his use alone.

The tragic life that Margarita Estrella was living out as Doña Dolores might never have ended, except that on one night life chose for her and everything changed. She was on her way home from meeting with yet another doctor, and her driver stopped her Mercedes at a busy street corner. The car was at a standstill, hemmed in on all sides by a long line of cars that seemed as if they would never move.

Margarita Estrella spotted a woman with two small children selling mangos and oranges under a streetlight. The

three were raggedly dressed, and it was apparent to anyone who saw them that they were tired after a long day of
peddling their goods and were now sitting quietly on the
sidewalk, their produce laid out before them.

Margarita Estrella noticed everything at once, then her
eyes lingered on the face of the boy, a child of about eight
years from what she could tell. She leaned closer to the
back window of the car and could hardly contain her joy,
for the child was a duplicate of her son Eduardo.

Had she taken a photo of the young boy and shown it to
her family, they would have sworn that Eduardo had been
born all over again. It was then that Margarita Estrella realized that her son Eduardo had died and would never
return to her again. She would never be able to explain to
anyone how she suddenly knew, but she did. Her heart
cried out to her that her mind's lie could not live any
longer. She had held the tears inside so long waiting for his
return, believing that one more search party would uncov-
er him and bring him home. And now this child's face, a
replica of her son's, rose before her in the busy street to tell
her that Eduardo would never come home.

Tears replaced all the lies, and Margarita Estrella held on
to the door's armrest as her body shook with violent sobs
that jerked her into reality. Her driver turned around
alarmed, fear rising as he looked at her crying so intensely
he felt she would die of sorrow. As he reached out one hand
to comfort her, inquiring what he could do, Margarita
Estrella opened the car door and in no more than two steps
was standing before the woman and two children. The
woman rose to her feet upon seeing the well-dressed lady
standing before her, tears in her eyes.

"Señora, how can I help you," she asked quickly.

"This child," Margarita Estrella said, pointing to the boy,
"Who is he?"

"He's my nephew, my sister's child. His mother and father died in a plane crash two years ago." The woman stared at Margarita Estrella, her look puzzled, her eyes questioning.

"His name?" asked Margarita Estrella excitedly.

"Eduardo," replied the woman, now holding the child's hand in her own.

With this, Margarita Estrella knelt on the rough pavement and embraced the child as if he were her own. The child put his arms around her neck. He had learned suffering and loss through his own life and understood Margarita Estrella's pain without even knowing he did.

"Would you allow me to take Eduardo home and see to his care?" she asked the woman. "Of course, I would have my driver take you home and give you every detail of where he will be."

"I see no problem in this, since he has no parents of his own to speak for him," said the woman. She considered that what this wealthy woman could give her nephew would be far more than what she could manage in a hundred lifetimes.

Not many hours into that night, Margarita Estrella's husband returned home to find his wife wearing a perfectly fitting blue satin dress that he didn't recall ever seeing before. Her hair was neatly pinned back and her face glowed, her radiant smile stunning him. So taken aback was he that his pipe fell out of his mouth and clattered onto the red-tiled floor.

"What is it?" he asked, afraid that perhaps his wife had truly gone mad.

"I have a surprise!" she responded happily. "Eduardo, come here!" she called.

For a second her husband expected to see a phantom appear; instead his eyes met those of his son Eduardo.

Seeing the young boy and his wife together made the elder Eduardo realize how much he had missed them both —his wife's radiant beauty and his son's manly, independent nature. The child approached the elder Eduardo and extended his hand, greeting him with respect.

"Eduardo Antonio, a sus órdenes, señor."

Not one thought of blackmail crept into the elder Eduardo's thoughts, which surprised even himself. The experience of seeing his son's face in the boy delivered up the tears he had so cautiously buried within and erased the anger he had held so long against his son, against the reckless ways that ended his life.

He was free once more. Free to be Margarita Estrella's husband. His power as a father also returned to him, the power he had left at his son's grave so long ago.

It was a night that was to last a lifetime for all three. The son who fell from the sky met the shooting star over the immense, dark sky of Mexico City. The glittering sky, every star brightly positioned in place, declared a truce with Margarita Estrella that night, ending the years of war.

BLACK WIDOW

A spider appearing under the kitchen sink wouldn't seem important unless you were the person who had to kill it.

Ever try to kill a black widow spider? The jet-black, overgrown spider with the red hourglass under its belly?

"A black widow bit your Abuelito," said Lydia's mother. "That's why he went blind. Yes, the spider bit him right on the forehead. He had the spot until he died."

"Black widow bites are worse than scorpion bites," said her Tío Leo while he jabbed his teeth with a toothpick after a big meal. "When you find the female, always look for her husband. He won't be far behind if she hasn't eaten him yet!"

"Watch those eggs," said Abuelita. "She's got eggs. I'll bet my last tortilla that spider has eggs, and just like any other mama she'll protect them. It's up to you to find them. Wonderful web she weaves," Abuelita added, looking up from her crocheting. "Wish I could do the same."

Can make you blind, worse than scorpions, look for the male, don't forget the egg sac. So much to remember besides the fact that they terrified Lydia and her daughter Jenny.

"Jenny, help me put the groceries away," Lydia said as she arranged the grocery bags on the kitchen table.

Just as she walked out of the kitchen, she heard her five-year-old screech, "A black widow, Mommy. Help!"

Lydia ran in expecting to see her child with a black widow stinging her and blindness beginning to set in.

Instead she found Jenny standing on a kitchen chair, hands to her mouth, screaming at the top of her lungs.

"Stop!" Lydia yelled, scooping Jenny up. "She won't jump at you, silly. Now stop!"

Jenny had been putting away a box of soap in the cabinet under the sink when she noticed the fine, silky web in one corner of the cabinet, outlined brightly by the light that invaded the darkness when she opened the door. Not wanting company, the black widow scurried away to hide in the darkest, uppermost corner of the cabinet's interior, invisible to the human eye.

The first thing Lydia did was to slam the cabinet door shut.

"There, we've got her trapped!" she exclaimed. She kissed her daughter on one chubby cheek. "Now go out to play and I'll kill the spider later."

"What if it gets away?" asked Jenny, her eyes filled with spider fear.

"Now, how will it do that? Is it strong enough to break the door down?" Then Lydia laughed and Jenny felt much better.

The question that came to Lydia's mind was how the black widow had gotten into the cabinet in the first place. There must be a hole leading to the outside. The black widow was clever enough to find the hole in the plaster and make its way along the pipes leading into the cabinet. This was a job for her father. She must remember to call him and have him come over and plaster over the hole and end the black widow invasion. For now it was up to her to kill the black widow, look for her mate, and eradicate the egg sac. Lydia looked at the groceries still scrambled over the kitchen table and determined to take care of it later that evening with the old lopsided broom she used for killing spiders, and the big sewer roaches that flew in the month of August.

Creepy crawling things didn't fascinate Lydia, especially when they resided right in her own apartment. The memory of her younger sister waving a black widow spider at the end of a stick made chills run down her back. Her sister collected black widows, thrilled by the danger of making them go where she wanted them to go, which was into a large glass jar she capped once she trapped them. And there were plenty to trap, living as they did in the hot Arizona climate. The spiders lived under old boards and in wooden storage rooms. Once in a while they found one under the sink or in a closet.

After putting Jenny to bed that night, Lydia stood, twisted broom in hand, facing the cabinet's open door. She took everything out of the cabinet. In one hand she held a flashlight. On the countertop within reach was a can of insecticide spray. She would first search out the black widow with the flashlight, saturate it with the spray to make it come out into the open, smash it with the broom, then look for her mate and the infamous egg sac.

Breathing deeply a few times, Lydia made the sign of the cross over herself and was glad no one was there in her small kitchen to see her hunting the black widow. What a picture this would make, she thought as she attempted a smile.

Lydia shone the beam of light into the cabinet corner, and almost immediately she spotted a gigantic black widow resting on its intricate web. She grabbed the can of insecticide and sprayed over and over again, watching the bottom of the cabinet where she figured the black widow would fall. Tenacious as always, the spider clung to its web, scurrying further up into the dark corner.

Lydia opened the kitchen door to let in some air, hoping to get out the strong odor of insecticide spray. Cool air filled the kitchen, and she motioned the bitter smell out the door with her hands.

Almost immediately Lydia sensed someone standing at the door in the dark night. She was ready to close the door when it swung wide open.

"Going somewhere?" asked Pete, now standing in full view at the door. He walked two steps into the kitchen.

Lydia's body prickled with fear, and her eyes reflected immediate terror. "Get out! she yelled. "Get out before I call the cops!"

"That old game?" answered Pete, drunkenly. "Cops don't scare me anymore. Not when my daughter's life is concerned."

Lydia watched his face. His eyes drooped and his lips curved in a cocky smile. "It's too late," she answered, gripping the handle of the broom tightly. "You had your chance, and the judge decided." Mentally, Lydia counted how far she was from the phone, and in one glimpse saw that no lights reflected from her neighbor's apartment. "This is no way to try to get custody of Jenny, Pete. You're only making things worse for yourself," she said, trying to reason with him.

"Nobody's gonna tell me what's enough!" Pete shouted, taking a step towards her. Lydia moved back, still grabbing the broom and lifting it up between them.

"Beat me with a broom, will you?" asked Pete, a sneer meeting Lydia's challenge. "You won't have to do too much as I don't plan to be around much longer anyway. That's why I came over, to see Jenny." He took a bottle of medication from the pocket of his jacket and held it up to Lydia's face.

"See this! That's what's gonna do me in, since my jefita

hid my gun. Then you'll pay for taking Jenny away from me." He opened the bottle and grabbed a handful of blue pills. He crammed them into his mouth, not waiting to chew but swallowing them whole.

"Stop it!" screamed Lydia, attempting to grab the bottle from Pete. He spun around and continued to eat the pills, grunting in rage.

Lydia dropped the broom, ran to the phone, and dialed 911. "My ex-husband's in my apartment and he's taking a whole bottle of pills!" she told the woman who answered.

"Does he have a weapon?" asked the woman.

"Nothing but the pills." Lydia told the woman her address then ran back to the kitchen to try to talk some sense into Pete. He stood at the sink beside the open cabinet door, gagging on the pills.

"Vomit them, you idiot!" she shouted, pounding on his back. She wished the black widow was out in the open so she could throw it in Pete's face and make an end of him if that's what he wanted.

Within ten minutes Lydia heard the blare of the fire truck racing to her apartment. Red lights flickered outside her window, and two paramedics marched in, grabbing Pete as he passed out on the floor.

Lydia stood by as they moved the unconscious Pete to the living room floor, taking his vital signs as they lay him down. She could hear the back-and-forth voices on their two-way radio outside her kitchen door and wondered how many neighbors that would attract.

Lydia looked at Pete in disgust. This was the lowest trick he had tried so far. Before this he had sworn he would move back to Mexico and no one would ever see him again, so he needed to say goodbye to Jenny for the last time. Lydia remembered letting him into the apartment. He had stayed the night, never even approaching his child's bed. A couple of times he had bribed her with money he knew she needed badly. With promises of giving her the money and leaving immediately, he had once again entered her apartment. He had stayed again for the night, fighting with her the next morning because she called him a liar. Obviously, he never gave her any money.

For two years he had used one trick after another to con his way back to Lydia, all the while never changing, never seeking peace with her.

"M'am, are you OK?" asked the paramedic. "You don't seem very upset."

"How can I be?" Lydia answered. "This is what I can expect from this man. I should have been more careful and not opened the door at all."

The paramedic looked toward the open cabinet. "You moving?"

"No," she said. "Something more important. I'm killing a black widow spider."

"Those things are nasty," he said in sympathy. "Deadly."

Lydia looked at Pete lying on the floor, seeming to be asleep, and she wondered who was more deadly.

"Ah, he's OK," said the paramedic filling out the chart. "He must have puked out most of the pills. What he needs is a good night's sleep. He's solidly drunk."

Lydia hesitated briefly to search out that one part of herself that always said yes when she meant no. "He won't sleep here," she said. "Throw him out on the street."

The paramedic laughed. "Well, we can't do that! But I'll tell you what. Give me the number of a family member and I'll tell them to come get him."

Lydia wrote down his mother's phone number on a piece of paper and watched as the paramedic attempted to talk to one, then to another voice, explaining the situation in simple sentences.

"Don't they speak English?" he asked, cupping the phone with his hand.

"Ask for his brother Eddie," she said.

With that, Lydia went back to the open cabinet in search of the black widow. She listened to the paramedic tell Eddie to come pick up his brother.

The second paramedic helped her shine the flashlight into the corner of the cabinet and she spotted the black widow again. "Move back," she told the man. "I can't miss or who knows where she'll go."

With one curving movement of the broom, fitting it perfectly into the corner, she brought the black widow to the bottom of the cabinet, sweeping it out to the kitchen floor. She immediately hit the struggling spider so hard with the broom that pieces of its black body got caught in the broom's spiny bristles. Then she checked the web and saw the emaciated body of the male already strung out on the web. Following the wavy line of the web, she located the egg sac suspended near the male's body. She dug her trusty, over-used broom into the web, destroying its intricate weave, and crushing the egg sac on the cabinet floor.

"Boy, you're good at this!" said the second paramedic in amazement.

"I have to be," answered Lydia. "I live alone."

"We'll wait until his brother gets here," said the first paramedic as he watched Lydia sweeping the remains of the black widow family out the door.

"I hate those things," he said, mimicking a shudder.

"I do too," said Lydia. "Especially when they invade my home."

Five minutes later Eddie knocked at the living room door and Lydia let him in.

"What have you done to my brother this time?" he asked between clenched teeth.

"Me?" asked Lydia innocently. "You mean what has he done to himself?"

"You have no mercy," Eddie said as he walked in to see his brother lying on the floor. "I swear, you're worse than a black widow."

Lydia couldn't help it. She laughed out loud. "Funny you should mention a black widow. I just finished killing one. Let me tell you something, your brother's poison is worse for me than any bite that stupid spider could ever give me."

"I don't know what my brother ever saw in you," Eddie said angrily.

"Probably an easy con," said Lydia.

Eddie glared at her, then looked away, studying his brother. Between the two paramedics and Eddie they were able to half-carry Pete to Eddie's car. Lydia didn't step out into the night, nor did she budge when she saw a few of her neighbor's faces already gathered under the streetlight.

As the paramedics and Eddie's car pulled out, Lydia slammed the door shut and double locked it. She stood amazed at herself, that this night her "no" had been stronger than Pete.

Putting the can of insecticide spray, broom, and flash-light away, Lydia closed the cabinet door with a bang and turned off the kitchen light. She made her way to her daughter's bedroom to check up on her, thankful that her child had slept through the whole incident.

"Mommy," Jenny asked sleepily, "Did you get rid of the black widow?"

"I got rid of the whole family," Lydia answered. "Go back to sleep. We're safe."

Then she made the sign of the cross over herself, bless-ing her victory.

LUCINDA MARÍA

Before Lucinda María was twelve years old, she had no problems at all. After she turned twelve, problems started. Her problems could be summed up in one word: men. Yes, the opposite sex troubled her immensely.

There was the time at Mary Lou's birthday party when her Tío Andrés pinched her cheek and bent down to kiss her right on the corner of her mouth. "Be prepared," he said, a half-drunken smile on his face. "Boys will be kissing you soon."

Before the party, Lucinda María played the jumping, running, and hiding games of childhood with abandon. After the party, she felt as though she had to watch how far she bent over if she was wearing a dress and how far forward she leaned if she was wearing a low-collared blouse. She didn't actually have breasts, but she could see the outline of their beginnings right through her clothes, which was why she started wearing her brother's T-shirts under her clothes, cutting along the high collars with a pair of scissors.

"Ma, I found two of my T-shirts all cut up," her stepbrother complained loudly. "Somebody must be using them as rags." Their mother looked them over quickly to see if they were dirty; she had no time to try to solve the mystery since they didn't need to be washed.

There were so many times Lucinda María wanted to run

to her mother and hide in her arms like she used to when she was younger. Nowadays her mother pushed her gently away, because she was rocking a smaller child to sleep or she was busy making tortillas or frying beans or searching for cobwebs in high corners of bumpy plastered walls with what was left of an old straw broom.

On summer evenings when the family gathered outdoors to talk or tell stories with friends and neighbors, Lucinda María sat on the grass next to her mother's chair and lay her head on her mother's lap. Her mother stroked her hair, her fingers running smoothly across Lucinda María's temple, arranging the fine, silky hair behind her ears. Her mother seemed softer at night, as if the day had pushed her around enough, and now the night could claim her as its own. The stars shone over their heads, and her mother counted them, telling Lucinda María if one was missing behind a cloud and how brightly their favorite one next to the moon was shining.

"I had hair as beautiful as yours," her mother said. "Long, red, and silky. I brushed it and brushed it until it shone like a new penny."

Then the problem started. "You baby her too much," said her stepfather. "Don't put all those things in her head. She'll be vain. She'll depend on her beauty instead of her brains."

Lucinda María's mother stopped stroking her daughter's hair just as Lucinda María closed her eyes and was ready to doze off in her mother's warm, squishy lap. "Ya, mi hija, go play with the others," her mother said. Lucinda María got up drowsy with the comfort of hands gently stroking and sat apart, ignoring the other children until her body returned to normal again.

Her stepfather's cigarrette burned, a tiny blazing ember in the dark night. Lucinda María saw his face reflected orange-red when he sucked on the end of it and looked at her. It seemed to Lucinda María that since Mary Lou's birthday party, her stepfather had joined the other men who looked at her daily with more and more interest. His eyes sometimes followed her around the house as she dusted under doilies and shook pillows. He pretended to sit in his chair the whole time reading his newspaper, but Lucinda María caught his eyes on her wherever she went.

When Lucinda María tried to leave the room, her stepfather would say, "You forgot that spot," or "You can't leave without dusting the pictures." The staring game would continue. Finally, her mother would call her and tell her she was needed in the kitchen.

After she turned twelve, Lucinda María was needed more and more inside the house to take care of her younger stepbrothers and sisters and to help her mother with cooking and cleaning.

When she passed by her stepfather to get to the kitchen, her arms tingled with goosebumps that told her she was afraid to pass by his legs outstretched in front of her. "Pardon me," she said with respect, for she knew better than to disrespect him, as it would mean big trouble for her mother. Sometimes he acted as if he wouldn't let her pass, and she had to jump over his legs. Lucinda María remembered sitting on his lap when she was young and going for a pony ride on his leg along with the other children. Now that she was twelve, she didn't dare even touch his leg.

One day when her mother was hanging out clothes to dry on a hot, breezy day, her stepfather called her into the living room. She saw newspaper thrown here and there all over the floor.

"Will you pick it up for me?" he asked. "I think the children must have been playing with it." Lucinda María looked into his eyes for an instant and noticed how they traveled the length of her body, from the collar of her flowered blouse to the summer shorts she wore and down to her legs and bare feet. Her face turned red, and she looked away not saying a word.

With his gaze burning through her, Lucinda María wanted only one thing and that was to pick up the newspaper as quickly as she could and run outside past this man who had changed into someone she didn't know anymore. After finishing the job, her stepfather offered her a quarter.

"You can reach into my pocket and get it yourself," he said, smiling nonchalantly as if another game was beginning.

"Give it to my mother, and she'll give it to me," Lucinda María said with her hands holding the newspaper in front of her.

"Now why would I want to do that?" he asked, one hand patting her head.

Without thinking Lucinda María cringed from his touch, her heart beating strong and wild, her hands suddenly cold. "You're still my little girl," he said as he tried to embrace her, crushing the newspaper. Just as Lucinda María was ready to let out a scream, her mother walked in with the plastic basket full of clothes that had dried in the sun.

"Help me fold these," she called to her daughter. Lucinda María ran past her stepfather, leaving him to pick up the newspaper she had dropped all over the floor. Her mother looked at her a few seconds more than she usually did. "What's wrong? Are you and Federico fighting?"

"No," she gasped.

Her mother looked past her at her stepfather then back to the basket of clothes.

"Let's get busy," she said, turning her back on him.

Federico was Lucinda María's older brother. Their father

abandoned them when they were toddlers, running away with their mother's best friend.

Lucinda María lost count of all the times her stepfather had made her mother remember that he had saved her from a fate of living from garbage cans. "Una trampa con hijos de nadie." After many hours of backbreaking work in fields and with pick and shovel on the hot, tar-slick streets, he had managed to save enough money to bring them to Tijuana, and pretty soon they would cross over as a family to Los Estados Unidos.

Federico, seventeen years old, already worked laying brick and laboring at construction sites with men twice his age. He traveled back and forth from Los Estados Unidos to Mexico. Sometimes he was gone for weeks at a time, leaving more space in the cramped house. It was during these times that Lucinda María felt even more afraid. Only when Federico was home did she feel safe.

Almost six feet tall, Federico towered over her stepfather, and the hours he spent at hard labor made his muscles bulge under his shirt and his shoulders broaden so much that their mother had to buy new shirts for him to wear. When he was there Lucinda María became bold and her stepfather became weak. He never played the staring games when Federico was around. Lucinda María noticed that he never had jobs for her to do when Federico was in the room. Instead he carried on long conversations with Federico about soccer, basketball, American football, bosses, and la migra.

And they laughed, two men together. Sometimes they drank beer or tequila, but Federico never got drunk because he respected his mother and knew how much she suffered for his sake. He had stood by her side when they had nothing to eat in the house but one tortilla that had to be shared three ways. He had been the one to give her a hug when he saw her crying at the table as she served bowls of soup made of leftover bones that she got from the butcher in exchange for cleaning out the mess of blood and guts that made his backroom look like a hundred animals had been slaughtered instead of two or three.

"Lucinda María, I want you to be careful with all these boys around here," Federico told her before he left again across the border. "They're trouble, the whole bunch of them, and want only one thing from you, even as young as you are."

It was all Lucinda María could do to contain herself and not cry out, "Stop him, stop my stepfather! It's him I'm afraid of, not the others."

Lucinda María shouted these words in her head but couldn't bring herself to say anything because she had no evidence to present. How could she endanger her mother's marriage, their home, all they were working for in the crazy, busy city of twisted, dirty streets that kept them enslaved day after day with the dream of Los Estados Unidos only a few steps away? Federico, so strong and able to work, so free, waved his hand from afar at Lucinda María. He was their one hope. With his increase in wages and his knowledge of English, they would soon be able to cross over, and little by little they would establish themselves in the country where everyone said life was fast and demanding but better, and with more money to be made.

Lucinda María might have continued longer in this unwelcome game of gazes and possession her stepfather played with her, if her friend Analisa had not spoken up for her one night.

Analisa was older than Lucinda María. She was fifteen and already she looked like the older girls that Lucinda María watched from the window of the school bus—young women dressed in perfectly matching outfits, every hair in place, heels clicking on harsh cobblestones, making their way to offices all around the city to work.

Analisa sat on the porch step next to Lucinda María in a white dress with a red belt and white shoes and a red bow that caught her dark brown hair at the nape of her neck. She stopped by to see Lucinda María after evening church services. Seeing the girls sitting on the step, Lucinda María's stepfather decided to go out to the front lawn to water the grass that looked as though an ocean of water would never revive it.

"Good evening to both of you," he said, smiling graciously, his eyes shifting from side to side.

"Good evening," answered Analisa. "Which reminds me that it's getting late and I have to get back home." She turned to look at Lucinda María and saw a look of alarm, an unspoken plea of "Don't go" in her friend's eyes.

Analisa hesitated, noticing that Lucinda María's large green eyes were luminous and frightened, as if a net had suddenly fallen around her. Without a word being spoken, Analisa understood the whole thing.

She said abruptly, "This grass looks quite dead, señor. Certainly any amount of water will be wasted on it."

"And what do you think I should do?" he asked, moving closer to the two girls.

"First of all, señor, if you truly want it to grow, you should never let it get as dead as it is now, for now you will have to spend twice as much time and energy trying to make it grow."

"Now, why didn't I think of that myself?" he said, smiling as if the most sensible answer he had ever heard had just been given. "And you girls look so grown-up yourselves that I could swear I was looking at two full-grown women. Two beautiful flowers growing in a perfect garden."

"Gardens were made by men, señor, but a woman, she is the prize creation of the Almighty," answered Analisa, tossing her hair back casually.

"And what does that make men?" he asked in a challenging tone.

"Only God can decide what each man is worth, señor, since it's He that reads hearts more surely and quickly than I'm reading yours right now," said Analisa.

At these words, Lucinda María stood up trembling on the wooden step. Lucinda María's stepfather threw the hose down and water gushed out haphazardly onto the small yellow lawn. He strode angrily toward Analisa, his short, bulky body stopping within inches of hers.

"Don't you dare talk to me like that, you little tramp!" he shouted at the top of his lungs.

And whether it was the liquor he drank earlier in the day, or whether the heat of the evening combined with the rising moon and his own lusts made him crazy, no one was to ever know. He grabbed Analisa by the shoulders and began shaking her hard, trying to push her down onto the wooden slats of the porch.

In the confusion of the moment Lucinda María screamed for help, her body flooding her mind with a panic she had never known before. She reached out as her stepfather struggled with Analisa and pulled at his shirt, scratching him with her nails, months of agony attacking him.

Lucinda María felt strong hands pulling her from her rage, separating her from the source of her attack. She spun around to stand face to face with Federico. In a flash of motion, he picked up his stepfather in one strong grasp and deposited him on the soggy lawn.

"And stay there, you filthy maniac," he shouted just as his mother and the other children ran out onto the porch.

Between the women and children crying and shouting,

and the two men fighting, one thing was certain, Lucinda María had faced her nightmare that night and her eyes weren't even closed. It was so unexpected that she almost didn't wake up, but then she heard Analisa telling Federico all about her fear. There was no place to run, for it was all out in the open, all out on the front lawn for everyone to see. Even the moon was an accomplice as it rose huge and yellow, shedding light on the whole scene, which was now filled with neighbors who wanted to find out why Lucinda María's stepfather was lying flat on his back on the wet, yellow grass.

Neighbors didn't say a word as Analisa cried out, "He's a pervert! A maniac that preys on children who have nowhere to run."

"You liar! You're telling nothing but stories!" he screamed. He stood up, brushing wet grass off his clothes. "Tell her, Lucinda María. Tell her the truth. You don't want to hurt your mother, do you?"

Lucinda María felt as if she were far away from home, as if she were watching all this in a movie and she didn't quite know what her next words should be. She looked at her mother, crying, at the frightened children holding on to her, at Federico, one arm around Analisa, so angry and fierce, and at her stepfather, arms open, hands pleading. "Explain it to them. Make it all right. You'll be to blame for everything."

Lucinda María looked at her stepfather. "I hate you for everything you've done to us. I hate you. I hope my mother leaves you. I hope you die!"

Lucinda María felt her mouth go dry. The dark night held onto her words then released them to the wind. The stars flickered light all about. Someone turned off the water from the hose and puddles on the lawn reflected wiggly lines of moonlight. Lucinda María's mother walked up to her daughter, her eyes filled with tears, and stroked her daughter's hair, holding her close. A peaceful drowsiness returned to Lucinda María, because she was half-child after all. On this night, her stepfather had nothing to say. Even the dead grass he had watered was more alive than he was.

(INDERELLA DAN(ED

Cinderella never danced as long and as hard as Virginia did when she was only six years old. There are pictures to prove it. It all began at her cousin Sara's wedding when she was the flower girl dropping rose petals every three steps and walking behind the fine, lace train that did a dive down her cousin's back. Even that procession was a dance for Virginia as she paced out the rhythm. One, two, three, petal. One, two, three, petal, all the way to the altar. When she looked back, she saw the red rose petals adorning the white carpet, and she felt satisfied that she had done her very best.

Later at the wedding dance, Virginia joined in la marcha. She ran along with the others, first in one line then another, holding hands, now making a long chain of London bridge is falling down, then prancing through the tunnel made of human hands, and finally ending up in a wide circle, watching the bride and groom dance a slow song all by themselves in the middle of the floor.

The photographer caught her and her big cousin Valentino—that's what everybody called him because he was such a ladies' man—dancing, and he held her hand high in the air and twirled her around like a ballerina. Virginia danced and everyone applauded her because she looked so pretty in her miniature wedding dress with her curls bobbing up and down and because she wasn't afraid like other kids to join in with the grownups.

Those who knew Virginia knew that she lived alone with her mother and father. She knew grownup stuff because that was all she had ever seen. As the years went by, no matter how patiently her parents waited and no matter how many promesas they made to saints and to God Himself, they never had anymore children. Virginia was destined to be one of a kind.

Virginia wakes up in her hospital room, having dreamed all night that she was dancing with her cousin Valentino even though she hasn't seen him in at least twenty years. She moves her fingers, one painful one after another, trying to stretch them out slowly. Next she moves her toes around slowly in the same way, and is glad she can still feel them, even though to do so is to feel pain. She knows that with diabetes sometimes the toes are the first to go, and any sign that they are still connected to her feet gives her comfort.

"How are we this morning?" asks the nurse standing over Virginia in a light blue uniform. "How are we doing?"

"Todavía viva," answers Virginia, hoping to dissuade further conversation.

In one quick motion the nurse opens the drapes and light floods into the room.

"Oh, look, what a bee-oo-tiful day we have!" she says loudly, forgetting that Virginia isn't hard of hearing. She speaks carefully, enunciating each word as if talking to a child. "You never know," she tells others. "These Mexicans act like they understand, but they don't."

Then she says brightly, "Your breakfast is almost ready," and hands Virginia a washcloth and a basin of warm water.

Virginia manages to dip the washcloth in the water,

passing the bar of soap briefly over it. She wrings out as much water as she can and slowly washes her face and hands. Finishing up, she folds the washcloth and sets it down on the nightstand along with the basin. She turns on the small radio that stands next to the alarm clock, and the Spanish station comes on the air, filling the room with voices and music.

Virginia is transported momentarily to her own wedding day when she danced with her husband in the center of a circle of family and friends. They danced slowly and romantically, she swaying with him, flowing with his every movement yet watching out for her cousin who was taking all the pictures. She wanted to be sure her best side showed in each picture. She is remembering how his hand felt at her waist when her breakfast arrives.

"Mrs. Rivera, breakfast is served." A new nurse comes in and uncovers the breakfast tray to reveal a watery mass that is supposed to be a soft-boiled egg, and dried toast alongside two small, plastic containers of butter and one of strawberry jelly. A piece of melon and a cup of coffee make up the rest of the meal.

"Not bad," says the nurse.

Virginia feels like saying, "Then why don't you eat it," but instead in broken English she says, "I like chorizo and papas for breakfas'."

"I'm sorry, I don't understand what that is," says the nurse, looking seriously at Virginia. "I'm sure you'll like this, though. It's good for you."

At her age, Virginia wonders if anything is good for her. She tries to eat a little, dipping the toast into the watery substance and trying to nibble around the edge. Juan will be upset if he hears I'm not eating, she thinks and manages to lift up the melon slice and bite off the very top. She knows that her son will check up on her and find out how much she's eating then reprimand her for not trying to get well.

"It's you, Mama, who are holding up the whole show," he'll say to her, glancing at his watch for the third time. "I'd take you home right now if it were up to me, but how will I know that you'll cooperate with us once you get home?" Then he'll lean over her and grab the phone from the night-stand, calling his office to find out if he has any more messages.

"Mi hijo el abogado," Virginia explained to her old friend Erlinda, who lived next door to her. "He's so busy. He has so many people who need him, he doesn't have time like he used to before."

Erlinda nodded her head in agreement, both of them knowing all along that Juan had never had time for his mother even before he became a big-time attorney. Of course, Erlinda's own son didn't even have the excuse of being an attorney. He only worked as a mechanic at the shop owned by his Tío Louie, and he still had no time for his mother.

"Sons are not like daughters after all," Erlinda reflected, thinking of her three daughters who visited her like clock-work. Of course, neither one of the three wanted to take her into her home, much less come to live with her.

"Someday I'll have to live with one of them," said Erlinda to Virginia as they sipped hot manzanilla.

"Who would you pick?" asked Virginia, buttering a piece of tortilla.

"None of them," said Erlinda, laughing, her false teeth gleaming. "They would end up running me out!"

Then they discussed horror stories of other women they knew who had ended up in their children's homes, living unhappily under the thumb of sons and daughters turned evil either from the influence of spouses or because they were tired of putting up with the inconvenience of caring for their aged parent.

Worse yet was the nightmare they faced when placed in a "rest home," or as Virginia and Erlinda called it, una casa para viejitos. To even think of such a place sent a shudder through the chubby frame of Erlinda and the sharp-boned frame of Virginia. "I'll run away first," said Virginia with conviction. "I swear I will."

"How?" asked Erlinda, "You can barely walk."

"I used to dance. Have you forgotten? I can take leg pain."

"That was years ago," answered Erlinda. "What now, Cinderella?"

"I'll manage," answered Virginia bravely.

And she had managed. She had managed to make her son and two daughters so upset with her that they voted to put her in a rest home whether she liked it or not. Erlinda was shipped off with her youngest daughter, and Virginia heard that her friend's prize roses were already overrun with weeds because her lazy grandson never stuck his head out the door except to see if it was day or night.

Everyone was so upset with Virginia, when all she wanted was to listen to the radio and tap her toes a little to the music.

"We're trying to sleep," her son said, coming into her room one night. "Look at the clock, Mama. It's one in the morning." He picked up the alarm clock and put it up to his mother's face. "See?"

"Go," said Virginia, "Go back to your gringa. God knows she would have never married you if you weren't a big-time attorney. What would your father say if he saw you tormenting me this way?" Then Virginia quieted down, because she had made her son come into her room.

She had seen him for five minutes at least. Now she could sleep.

"Has my son called tonight?" Virginia asks the nurse who comes into her room with her medicines.

"I don't think so, but I can check," says the nurse, writing down information on a pad of paper.

Virginia longs to talk to someone, anyone, who understands a little Spanish, but no one does except for the old priest who comes by every other day to give her Holy Communion. He only stays a few minutes, and of course it's not like talking to another woman, her friend Erlinda for instance.

He's probably mad at me again, figures Virginia as she turns up the radio a bit. "Solamente una vez se ama en la vida," sings the radio. The old song brings memories to Virginia of her first dance, with a man her father hated. A man who was taboo for her, forbidden fruit.

He was usually dangling out in front of her when she and Erlinda walked back from their jobs at the laundry. He was sitting in front of a small frame house, listening to an old radio. No one knew whether he had a family or not, because he worked the fields with the other braceros who came over in droves each season to pick cantaloupes, watermelons, lettuce, grapes, and whatever else grew in the hot, dusty fields. He was short and broad-shouldered, with a mass of curly hair and a moustache that dipped below his lips, framing his mouth in an upside-down smile.

He always dressed casually in a simple T-shirt, khaki pants, and work boots, and he acted like he hardly noticed the girls as they passed by.

Usually he was busy adjusting the radio. Sometimes he

was standing in the doorway dancing with an imaginary partner. His not noticing went on for two weeks, maybe less, then one day he looked at Virginia and said, "Do you know how to cha-cha-cha?"

"Me?" answered Virginia. "I've been dancing since I was six."

"Show me," said the man, his smile curving his moustache up.

And as Erlinda watched in horrified glee, Virginia danced right there on the dusty, hard ground with a stranger who was taboo.

He could dance, Virginia remembered, with more rhythm than any man she had ever known. As they cha-cha-cha'd back and forth, teasing one another, chasing forward and backward, he whispered something in Virginia's ear. Erlinda didn't hear what it was. Virginia never forgot. "Come back later."

It was a statement that carried more than his desire to dance with her. It was a command that repeated itself in Virginia's mind over and over again, yet she never told Erlinda. For this reason, Virginia had one less regret to face.

On the night she returned, she lied to her parents and slipped away to bed early, hoping they wouldn't check up on her. Escaping by way of a window, Virginia jumped out silently into the night, making her way down the alley as far as she could go and crisscrossing two open fields until she came to the house of the man with the radio. His name no longer existed in Virginia's memory, for he was part of all she had danced out of her life.

The night they danced, the man held her close each time a waltz was played. Virginia was so caught up in the rhythm and beauty of his fluid movements that she didn't feel too uncomfortable with his body next to hers and his breath at her ear.

Virginia had heard the story of Cinderella and her Prince Charming, and dancing with this stranger under the moon and stars with a breeze just barely blowing her waist-length hair, she felt every bit a princess herself. As the night grew late, Virginia began to feel as if her coach wouldn't wait, and she could almost hear the clock striking midnight when the man invited her in to have a drink of lemonade. Once inside, Virginia learned that the man knew more than how to dance. Pressing eager hands on her, the music blaring outside his house, he didn't let her go until the clock struck its last chord and the dress she wore had turned to rags. Virginia crisscrossed the two open fields and ran down the alley back to her house, losing both glass slippers as she made her way through the window and back into bed, shivering and shaking from fear.

She knew something had happened to her that should never have happened. Everything was all wrong inside her. The cells of her body regrouped themselves, creating someone she didn't know. Her arms, hands, and legs didn't know each other anymore.

Erlinda never knew why Virginia chose another route on their way to and from work, refusing to pass by the small frame house of the man with the radio.

For months Virginia sat apart in the evenings wondering about this thing that had happened to her. She knew it had something to do with men and women, for blood is not easily shed and certainly marks the end of something, or at least the beginning of something new.

Before long Virginia turned back to the dance. This time it was a sad, mournful dance she did all by herself in her room. She twirled and turned, one hand reaching up, the other coming down, both arms making a circle that had no end. The dance reacquainted her hands with her legs. It reunited her head and heart and stretched out her spine down the length of her back. It lingered inside her, whispering, shushing her like a baby. She became her own lullaby.

Her parents never knew, nor did Erlinda. Virginia told it only to the dance, to the movements that ruled her body. Virginia waited as she danced, and she didn't know for what. Maybe if she hadn't danced as long and as hard, she would have returned to the man with the radio, or maybe she would have told her mother what had happened. But the dance was alive, more real than anyone else.

The day came when the mournful dance that possessed Virginia began to teach her hope, and she looked out at the evening sky and realized that everything was the same. Her graceful movements had filled up what was lost, and she was Virginia again, with one more dance learned, ready for real love, open, alarmed, in awe because something could be taken away then given back.

In her darkened room, Virginia hears the faint chatter of nurses in the hallway. She lies back on her bed and lets the dance start all over again, except this time she doesn't move her swollen legs. Instead Virginia depends on the dance to guide her in the dark, her faithful partner dancing gently with her in silence.

THE DANGEROUS GAME

Sofía didn't hear the knock at the trailer's door, but her sister did. "Stevie Boy's here," Martha said, peering into the dark bedroom. On the bed, Sofía turned to face her sister's voice, instinctively covering herself against the chilly night air.

"Oh no," she moaned. "Now I'll have to get up." She threw the blanket off and sat up reaching for her white shawl to wrap herself into. She was still wearing the dark blue shorts and striped midriff top she wore earlier in the day. Gold earrings dangled almost to her shoulders.

"Might as well blend in with the general population," she had said to Martha as they boarded the car heading towards the Gulf of Mexico. "Gold earrings are big on the other side."

The three-and-a-half hour drive from Phoenix to Puerto Peñasco had been nondescript until the travelers hit the shimmering scene of white sandy shores set against the crystalline, blue-green waves of the Sea of Cortez. Then it was all worth it. Every moment of the three days Sofía spent in the rented trailer at La Playa Del Sol with her older sister Martha and her seven-year-old son Frankie imbedded itself in her memory like a movie she could play back at will.

Even before unpacking, Sofía and Frankie were already running up and down the shoreline, bare feet making prints all over the wet sand. Sofía greeted the ocean like a long-lost lover she embraced over and over again, holding and caressing, making up for the time spent apart.

"Stevie Boy won't wait forever!" said Martha, impatiently watching her sister as she sat up in bed. "I want to know everything he tells you. This is just too good to be true," she said, trying not to laugh too loud.

Estevan, last name unknown, had been christened "Stevie Boy" by Martha when the two women had giggled over his reaction to seeing Sofía standing in front of him on the beach. "Love at first sight!" teased Martha. "Did you see the guy? He looked like he had been hit on the head by a two-by-four! He was ready to drop at your feet!"

"Don't exaggerate," answered Sofía, amused by her sister's description. Yet she wondered about "Stevie Boy" and how he had gazed into her eyes, connecting in a second with some secret, unmarked part in her that made her struggle a bit to keep her composure. The wind helped her just then because she turned her head to smooth back waves of her long dark hair and was able to break from his gaze. Now he was here. Estevan, waiting for her on the trailer's dark patio. Just to talk.

Stepping out in bare feet, wrapped in her shawl, Sofía barely made out the sound of the ocean's waves. Under the light of a quarter moon she saw the outline of rocks on the shore as the tide shifted out to sea.

"Please sit down," she said, pointing to one of the vinyl-covered lounge chairs. Estevan took her hand briefly as she sat down and would have held on to it had Sofía not pulled it back, securing both hands under her shawl.

"Are you cold?" he asked.

"Just a little," she said, noticing how the light from one of the outdoor lamps reflected on his face. The light outlined his neatly shaven beard and moustache. She couldn't see his eyes as clearly as in daylight, but even in the dark they seemed able to reach her and set a course that Sofía was already beginning to dread.

Wasn't it enough that the ocean had already filled her with its secret message? Earlier in the day, as the ocean's restless waves had crashed to shore around her feet, Sofía had heard its voiceless tones within herself: "Learn from me. Learn to know the changes you must make. Watch my moods and learn your own." Sofía had silently studied the creasing and uncreasing of the waves, delighting in the play of sunlight on its blue and green hues. Learn? Learn what? This was vacation time. She had left all her energy in the city, and here by this splendid sea she could rest, putting the demands of her career in the farthest corner of her mind. Now this man sat close by her in the dark, demanding something of her.

"I haven't been able to stop thinking about you since I first saw you on the beach," he said in a matter-of-fact tone.

"Now, why would that be?" she asked. She felt flattered, but then again, words would demand something of her, and her strength had been left behind. She suddenly wished she had sent Martha out to tell him she was asleep.

"I've looked for a woman like you all my life. A woman beautiful in body, and most important, beautiful within." He bent towards Sofía. "When I saw you running up and down the shore, playing with the waves, I thought I was looking at a goddess! It was then I decided I had to know who you were."

"Living out here you must see beautiful women all the time," said Sofía. "I don't think I'm more beautiful than others you've seen." She was aware of his eyes studying her face. He seemed to be taking in the details of her large brown eyes and smooth skin. Every movement of her hair as the wind blew gently through it seemed of special interest to him. He reminded Sofía of a crazed teenager in love for the first time, stumbling over his feet to get to the side of his beloved.

"How long have you lived out here?" she asked.

"All my life. My father was a fisherman. Los camarones—you've seen our giant shrimp? Back in the old days they were even more plentiful than they are now. The pollution in the water has reduced their numbers, which has affected our whole town."

"So you're a fisherman?"

"You might say it's in my blood, but I've also attended the university and taught in las escuelas secundarias, which are like the high schools in Los Estados Unidos."

"Have you ever traveled to Los Estados Unidos?"

"No, I never have. And frankly, I don't think I want to. I don't like the fast way people live over there. Americans live under pressure and don't even know that their very lives are the price for such a pace. Give me the tranquil life and a woman like you and I would live like a king!"

Sofía looked past him to the distant, dark shore, avoiding his eyes. All around them people were settling down for the night. The other trailers had their lights out, and only one or two people lingered peacefully on the beach. Sofía's restless mind prepared a description of the scene: "Well, you see, this guy fell in love with me right there on the beach. You should have seen how his face and body changed in front of my eyes. Of course he can't speak English, and doesn't know a thing about what I do in the States."

And everyone she knew would say she had lost a screw somewhere in the sand at Peñasco and would she please come to her senses and stop tempting fate with this mojado from Mexico. How would she explain him to the empty, sophisticated people that smothered her life with their superficiality?

"Dangerous little place, Puerto Peñasco," Sofía said. "I mean for the ships that come into port. I imagine ships might crash up against these rocks in stormy weather."

"Oh, absolutely," Estevan answered. "It lives up to its name. But then again every port has its dangers, not unlike love, I suppose."

"Now, that's something I would agree with you about," said Sofía enthusiastically.

"So, you've loved someone?"

"Why do you think I come to this place? I loved someone and it never brought me anything but pain. I come here and let the ocean wash all the pain out of me, and so far every time I come more of the pain is taken away. I'm feeling better all the time."

"What about loving again? Have you tried that?" he asked, his voice raised slightly.

A shudder that had nothing to do with the ocean breeze went through Sofía. "No, that's too dangerous for me. It's like trying to find my way back to port in the dark. The pain of crashing against the rocks would be too much for me."

"You would then stay out in the dark ocean all night? Wouldn't that be more dangerous?"

"Nothing's more dangerous than love," Sofía whispered. Her voice sounded strangely distant to her.

"Will you ever be ready for love again?" Estevan asked as he tenderly reached over to reposition Sofía's shawl on her shoulders. "Being ready is not really falling in love. It's just saying, I need to love again for my own good."

Sofía sensed a mighty ocean wave crashing within her, and she answered angrily, cutting off his touch with one shrug of her shoulder. "You have no idea what I've been through! No idea at all!"

She shifted restlessly in her chair, uncomfortable with his words and with the touch of his hands on her shoulders. An impulse went through her to get up, end the crazy seaside conversation, and go inside to sleep; yet anger demanded too much strength from her, and she felt too tired and helpless to let it have its way.

"Are you afraid of love?" Estevan asked quietly, not responding to her anger.

"I didn't say anything about being afraid. I said it's too dangerous for me. There's a difference, you know."

"Danger provokes fear, I suppose," he said, smiling casually. "But then what do I know about love?"

At this Sofía also smiled, because looking at Estevan, tan and muscular, sitting moonstruck beside her seemed so ridiculous to her. He didn't know the first thing about her. It wouldn't take long for him to find out just how dangerous she was in the game of love. She could send a man careening like a madman after her, following the trail that led to her only to find that she was positioned behind a locked gate. Maybe she should send him down the dead-end trail just to stay in practice, just to see his passion burn for nothing, because the way he was looking at her now sent a message of sheer desire, of a pure need to encircle her in his arms. His need to touch her hung in the air and became an urgent, unspoken request that she understood as easily as she understood the ocean's voice. Yet she would not allow herself to answer.

Gazing out into the ocean's dark void, Sofía remembered that other dark void she had stared into, knowing there was one other person there she had to confront. She shouldn't have followed her husband that night. But truth needed to make itself known, and it was more powerful than she was.

In the end Sofía saw her—the woman who was with her husband in the dark bedroom. She materialized, moving like a phantom towards Sofía until they were almost face to face.

"She's nothing to me," said Rigo to the carelessly dressed white woman who now stood before them both. "I tell you, she's nothing to me!" he cried again, pointing to Sofía.

"Who are you?" the woman asked.

"I'm his wife," Sofía said over Rigo's shouts. "He should park his car somewhere else and you should remember to lock your door."

"His wife?" asked the woman, honestly surprised, "But I thought . . ."

Rigo's shouts of denial and mockery rose in pitch.

"Shut up!" the woman shouted at him. "Shut up and get the hell out of here!" Her voice sounded loud and coarse in the night.

Sofia stood between Rigo and the woman, unwilling to believe he had violated her clean love for this. She felt like a helpless child standing on a wooden crate, peering at something sinful and forbidden. Explanations had never been enough for Sofía after that night, even though Rigo called hundreds of times, blaming himself for being too drunk to know better.

"What's important to me is you," Estevan was saying. "In a relationship, the other person must be of utmost importance. Then the couple will be balanced." After a pause he added, "I'm having trouble right now because I get distracted watching you, but if I were to think about you while away from you, I could tell you exactly why I feel the way I do."

"Yes, I suppose men can say just about anything they want," said Sofía. "Then when a real test comes, they abandon, they deny."

"Again, love can't be measured that way," answered Estevan. "One denial today might mean total fidelity on another. Haven't you heard of St. Peter and his denial of Christ? Yet he became the leader of the Church."

Anger rushed through Sofía like an underwater current out of control. "It's easy to say that, but hard to live! Usually if someone can't be trusted they stay that way."

"You must have really been hurt by someone," said Estevan, his voice dropping to a deeper tone. "I'm sorry it's been that way for you, but will you always be closed to love?"

Again the question and the ocean's demand collided in Sofía's mind. "Learn to understand your moods and changes," whispered the ocean's waves. Words caught in Sofía's throat, a hurricane brewing behind her closed lips. She wanted to yell, "You sit there asking me to do something you know nothing about! Just like all men, always asking and never giving!"

Sofía reached inside herself for the old angry energy, but found it evaporating in the cool ocean breezes, leaving her gasping for something to fill up the spaces. If not anger, then what? The pain had to be relieved one way or another.

"Are you listening to me?" asked Estevan, putting one hand on Sofía's shoulder. "Love isn't that hard to come back to."

"I already told you, it's too dangerous for me." Sofía's eyes closed in a weariness that had nothing to do with the late hour.

"You don't have to jump into love like you jump into the ocean."

Sofía closed her eyes. She felt another void opening around her. A blindness gathered in her eyes, and a darkness worse than her husband's treachery closed in upon her. Silently she cried out against the void, seeing herself stranded and alone far out in the dark ocean. Would she ever be ready? She opened her eyes to see a look of absolute worship on Estevan's face. The part of herself that would have been angered by such a look was gone.

"I need to go in," she said, standing up. Her shawl fell at her feet, and Estevan picked it up in one smooth, even motion, arranging it around her again. Then he raised one of Sofía's hands to his lips and kissed it gently.

Sensing the dangerous approach of love, Sofía ran inside, determined to leave Estevan frozen in position, his hand reaching out for hers.

"What's going on?" asked Martha drowsily as Sofía closed the door behind her.

"Nothing," said Sofía, now safe from a raging storm.

"Where's Stevie Boy?"

"Outside, playing dangerous games."

"Join him, why don't you?"

"Maybe tomorrow," said Sofía. She threw off her shawl and checked for bruises.

ONCE FOR PEPITO

"Mama," Pepito asked, "are oceans where whales are found, or do they live in rivers?"

"Oh, in oceans of course, Pepito," answered his mother, Angélica. "They're much too big to live in rivers. Why, their huge bodies would pop out of the water and pretty soon they would die."

"I'd like to ride one someday," said Pepito, "but I don't think I can get to the ocean. What do you think, Mama? Could I ever get to the ocean? And if I did, would I find a whale that would give me a ride?"

Angélica thought about the ocean, remembering the dolphins she often watched bathing in foamy, frothy water, diving in as easily as though the water was a misty cloud. Now, how to get Pepito to the ocean, for under the circumstances even this request had to be considered. Perhaps Tío Sabio would come in handy. He would be willing to help. But would there be time?

After giving Pepito all his medicines that night, his mother helped him remove the beautiful blue cap she had made for him by crocheting bright blue threads into straight, tight lines that hardly showed his hairless scalp at all. Then she bent down and gently kissed Pepito's swollen head, carefully pressing her fingers against the scars that formed ridges in three places.

She kissed him and hugged him over and over again—

at least ten times—before laying him in his little bed, for she was never sure which night would be the last one for hugs and kisses. Then she covered him with the colorful woolen blanket she had bought for him at the marketplace.

In the light from the room's small lamp and the veladora that burned before the crucifix, Pepito's ashen face took on a look of holiness, as if he had already left his stricken body. To his mother he resembled a baby bird who was so weak he could not even move to the edge of the nest. His feathers had long since dropped away, and he was left with fine bones showing and large, gray eyes that remained deep in thought no matter where he looked.

They both knew, although neither said anything, that the other was hurting more than words could describe. So Pepito managed a smile and said, "I love you, Mama."

On this night Angélica's tears fell in spite of all she did to hold them back, and she said, "I'll love you forever, mi hijito." Her lips trembled with emotion as she gently held her child's body.

Then they both prayed a simple prayer asking God to continue to bless Pepito and, when it was time, to take him far away to a place where Pepito would never feel such pain again.

That night Pepito had a wonderful dream. He dreamed about whales. He saw their glorious black-and-white bodies moving over the water as easily as he had once moved his body through the air. He hopped on top of one that bowed its back for him to climb on. Suddenly an exhilarating feeling of strength exploded in his body, and he and the whale moved in perfect harmony over the glistening water. So much strength made his head spin. He was drunk with the sun and the surf and the sheer force of the whale's body as it thundered under his legs. Never had he felt such power!

As Pepito slept and dreamed about whales, his mother hurriedly slipped a shawl over her shoulders and rushed out onto the dirt road that shone in the moonlight like a white satin ribbon. She ran down a short stretch of uneven ground to Tío Sabio's small house.

"Tío Sabio! Tío Sabio!" she called loudly as she knocked on the rough wooden door.

Tío Sabio opened the door immediately, expecting the worst.

"Is it over, Angélica?" he asked anxiously as he scanned his niece's face. His fingers were already running nervously through his gray hair.

"No. ¡Dios guarde la hora!" Angélica answered.

Then she asked, "Is there any chance you might take Pepito and me to the ocean tomorrow? He wants to ride on the back of a whale."

"My dearest," said Tío Sabio, "I may be able to take you to the ocean, but as for a whale ride, I don't quite know how I will do that. My power ends at the shoreline."

"God will provide," said Angélica. Then she turned and ran back into the dark night.

Arriving breathlessly back home, Angélica walked quickly to Pepito's room. His room, separated from her own by a narrow hallway, was left with its door open so she could check up on her son throughout the night. She walked silently in and was stunned to see Pepito's face wearing a peaceful, joyful expression. Indeed, his face resembled that of an angel. Amazed, she thanked God for the relief from pain granted to her son.

Upon saying her prayer of thanksgiving, Angélica was struck with how her conversations with God had changed over these many months, from shaking an indignant finger in His face at seeing her only child die, to allowing herself to count as miraculous every moment she and Pepito spent together. She discovered that as she pleaded for her son's recovery, it was herself she was really praying for, and she saw how selfish she was to ask over and over in her dark room, "Why me? What have I done to deserve this?"

In the past she had found herself begging not only for her son's health, but that she would be spared his death. Yes, she even had prayed that the child's disease would miraculously leave his body and enter her own, if indeed sacrifice was what God demanded. And her anger had risen in vicious fury, defying the darkness around her, challenging God to come down from His throne and talk to her face to face if He dared!

The pain of her grief had grown as she thought of her young husband dying in a senseless accident at the mines, and it seemed to Angélica that there was never a woman so filled with torment as she was. Pain entered her like a furious blow to her stomach. It traveled through her body, owning her like an unseen hand, touching her in the dark. Then a fitful sleep would fall upon her, and the night would grant her a bit of rest, though barely enough for her blurred mind to envision waking again.

Yet on this night, within seconds of laying her weary head on her pillow, Angélica also began to dream. She dreamed that Pepito had been born all over again. She saw him clearly, as big as he was now yet somehow also like a newborn, for his flesh was soft and unblemished by disease. He looked radiantly at her as she held him in her arms, and though newly born, he spoke and laughed like an older child. Angélica's heart almost burst with joy to see her son so exhuberantly happy. His father was standing beside her, gazing lovingly at both of them.

Perhaps the dream was too joyous a thing to contain.

Angélica woke in the dark, her heart beating wildly. For an instant or two she completely forgot that her son was anything less than the young, vibrant child she had just dreamed about and that his father was anything less than alive and coming home to her after a long day's work.

For that brief instant, Angélica thanked God for the health of her son and for the strength of her husband who was able to provide for all their needs. Then as quickly as the relief and peace came, it was gone, leaving her in a huge black hole of pain as she remembered how things really were.

She rolled out of bed, falling to her knees on the bare concrete floor and, reaching out with one hand, closed her bedroom door to prevent Pepito from hearing her. She bent her head to the floor's rough surface, and her tears fell like torrents of water that have been held back too long at the site of a great dam. She wept and wept until her heart told her it was enough.

Angélica rose from her knees that night strangely strengthened, although to the human eye things were still the same. She wiped her tears for the last time, her heart satisfied that Pepito's joy was secure and that his strength would endure forever.

The next day early in the morning, Tío Sabio came over in his old faded pickup truck, the one with a piece of metal sticking out of the steering wheel that Tío Sabio used as a gear shift. He honked the horn twice just like he always did. Once for Angélica and once for Pepito.

Angélica had already wrapped Pepito in his colorful woolen blanket to protect him from the chill air of morning. He had taken a few sips of hot chocolate and eaten just a corner of pan duro so he wouldn't vomit when the nausea hit him. His scarred head was well covered by the perfectly fitting blue cap.

"Come in, Tío Sabio," said Angélica happily. "Come enjoy a delicious cup of hot chocolate with cinnamon before we go out looking for whales."

"Ah, chocolate, always my favorite," answered Tío Sabio, rubbing his calloused, arthritic hands together for warmth. "And how is my dearest Pepito today?" he asked. "Ready to ride on the back of a whale, are you?"

Pepito's eyes, sunken and gray, looked out from the blanket at Tío Sabio. His voice was unusually clear for one so weak.

"Oh, yes, Tío Sabio, I dreamed about whales last night and I rode on the back of the biggest one!"

"You must teach me to ride one," Tío Sabio said, smiling.

The three sat together on the front seat of Tío Sabio's old pickup and rode three hours to the beach. Angélica didn't forget Pepito's medicines, although she didn't think he would need them that day. Gray clouds hung low and billowing. In some spots the sky could be seen deep blue in the crisp autumn morning. As they traveled, Tío Sabio whistled a happy tune, and Angélica sang, "Naranja dulce, limón partido, dame un abrazo que yo te pido." This was Pepito's favorite song, and he joined in the chorus with one or two words at a time as he struggled for breath.

Every now and then his mother bent down and kissed Pepito on the head, even lifting the beautiful blue cap to see and caress that which Pepito could not bear to see himself—the mutilations he had received. Tío Sabio turned the rearview mirror onto its side so there would be no chance of Pepito even catching a glimpse of his own reflection.

Pretty soon the three could smell the ocean in the air. Whether it was the wind that had picked up or the gaiety and music that issued from the unusually large crowds that lined the sandy shore, no one knew, yet something made

Pepito sit up between his mother and Tío Sabio. This he had not been able to do for a whole year at least.

"There's a whale here!" he shouted. His mother and Tío Sabio jumped at the sound of his voice, which they hadn't heard so loud and strong since the day the doctor had said, "Pepito will not live to see his eighth birthday."

Tío Sabio stopped the pickup truck, and Angélica jumped out, flinging her slender body into the currents of wind that were blowing everywhere.

"Whale! Whale!" the people were shouting. "Look at the size of it! Look at its grandeur! Can anything equal its beauty?"

And far in the distance, Angélica caught the glint of the sun shimmering on an immense black-and-white mound that balanced itself on the ocean's waves like a floating island, rocking back and forth, now appearing, now disappearing.

In his excitement, Tío Sabio had already picked up Pepito in his arms and was running toward the sea. Angélica saw Pepito's blue cap bobbing over Tío Sabio's shoulder as she ran full speed after them.

Breathless, Tío Sabio reached out to the ocean's bond with earth and allowed the waves to come up around his shoes and up his pant legs. Beside him Angélica waded in, huaraches and all, heedless of the water soaking her skirt.

"Pepito, mi hijito, querido! she cried, "God has sent you a whale!"

As her words sounded in the wind, the immense whale appeared to face the three. The whale moved as if its direction were set, gracefully gliding in a straight course toward Pepito.

Pepito threw off the woolen blanket and positioned himself upright in Tío Sabio's arms. As the whale approached closer and closer, the crowd cowered in fear, not understanding why the giant creature would come so dangerously close to humans, yet there it was, almost motionless.

"Perhaps it's ill!" cried someone in the crowd.

"Perhaps it will deliver a baby!" cried another.

But neither was right, for the whale bowed its towering body ever so slightly before the frail child. Tío Sabio reached out his arms as far as they would go, and Pepito put out his hand and touched the whale's sleek, glistening head, so unlike his own lacerated one. In that moment Angélica saw Pepito's eyes fill with pure joy, and the smile she remembered from the dream once again shone on his face. Then Pepito's head fell to his shoulder never to rise again.

Pepito took off on the whale. Dipping and spinning, the giant creature spewed white water into the air, joyously remembering ancient times, when every boy in the whole wide world rode a whale at least once in his life.